ENGAGING EMERSYN

RAPTOR
BOOK 9

PJ FIALA

COPYRIGHT

Publisher's note: This is a work of fiction. Names, characters, places, and incidents either are the product of the author's imagination or are used fictitiously. Any resemblance to actual events, locales, or persons, living or dead, is entirely coincidental.

Printed in the United States of America

First published 2022

Fiala, PJ

ENGAGING EMERSYN / PJ Fiala

p. cm.

1. Romance—Fiction. 2. Romance—Suspense. 3. Romance - Military

I. Title – ENGAGING EMERSYN

ISBN-13: 978-1-959386-16-2

GLOSSARY

Read the prequel to RAPTOR - RAPTOR Rising here. https://www.pjfiala.com/books/RR-BF

A Note from Emersyn Copeland:

Founder of RAPTOR (Revenge And Protect Team Operation Recovery).

I was wounded when my convoy hit an IED and retrained through OLA (Operation Live Again) to perform useful services for the military; mainly locating missing children. Empowered by the work but frustrated by governmental limitations, I contacted my father Dane Copeland and my Uncle Gaige Vickers, GHOST's leader, to form a covert group not restricted by governmental regulations, consisting of highly trained post military men and women with injuries and disabilities. Our offices are housed on the GHOST compound. I divided RAPTOR into three teams of expertly trained individuals who were selected for their specific abilities. Let me introduce you to the Teams.

Team Alpha: Recon and Recovery:

Diego Josephs: Former Army Recon expert. Friend of GHOST Josh Masters. Recent retraining for OLR (Operation Live Again). Demonstrative and possessive, he is a team player battling PTSD.

Ted: Diego's Therapy and service dog. A mix of black lab and Newfoundland.

Donovan "Van" Keach aka the "Reformer": Completed OLR with Emersyn. Blinded in his left eye during a military operation. Out spoken, opinionated, daredevil with a strong belief in service and a mission for justice no matter the risk.

Charlesia "Charly" Sampson: A friend of Emersyn's Aunt Sophie. Medically discharged after she lost her left arm at the elbow during a mission in Afghanistan. Tough adaptable, independent sarcastic, and determined but self-conscious of her appearance. Excels in disarming and getting people to trust her and ferreting out information.

Team Bravo: Cyber Intelligence:

Piper Dillon: Attractive and energetic with a ready smile but all business. Expert computer hacker, communications device expert and internet guru.

Caiden Marx: Strong and independent, Caiden suffered lung damage while serving due to an explosion and fire. He struggles to breathe and can't take on energetic tasks but excels on Team Bravo and has unique hacker abilities.

Deacon Smythe: Deacon has a ready smile and is always happy but takes his job seriously. He's an expert on computers and communications.

Team Charlie, Special Ops:

Falcon Montgomery: Son of Ford Montgomery, a GHOST team member, Falcon lost hearing in his right ear. Growing up with Ford, Falcon is a natural in special ops, and willing to go the extra mile to get the job done.

Creed Rowan: Former SEAL, well rounded in terms of skill, Creed's specialties are explosives and swimming. His abilities take him places others don't dare go.

Emersyn Copeland: Daughter of GHOST founder, Dane Copeland and niece to current GHOST owner, Gaige Vickers, Emersyn's strengths are in business and extracting her staff member's special talents. But, she's equally good at ferreting out suspects' deep dark secrets.

House Staff:

Sheldon Daniels, Cook: Former military, Marine. Friend of GHOST's house keeper and cook Mrs. James. Demands order in his kitchen, punctuality and the keeper of all secrets, bonus he's a damned good cook.

Shioban O'Hearn, Housekeeper: Sassy mid- thirties housekeeper. Loves the thrill of working with badasses, but doesn't let herself get walked on.

DEDICATION

I've had so many wonderful people come into my life and I want you all to know how much I appreciate it. From each and every reader who takes the time out of their days to read my stories and leave reviews, thank you.
My beautiful, smart and fun Road Queens, who play games with me, post fun memes, keep the conversation rolling and help me create these captivating characters, places, businesses and more. Thank you ladies for your ideas, support and love. The following characters and places were created by:

Emersyn Copeland - Nikkita Marie Blake
Lia Landon - Abigail Capps
Chase Nicholas - Deb Jones Diem (Chase) Theresa Sollecito Natole (Nicholas)
Drake Nicholas - Lynne Kerr
Nicola - Nancy Hoch
Neve (Victoria Andrews) Patterson (Belinda Jackson Hercule)
Isaac Blair - Mary Lou Melzer

Louise - Jayne Smith
Calum Reid - Yolanda Tobiasen
Dr. Karol Ember - Kathy Franklin
Quinn - Eva De Gracia

Cartwright's Pass - Lyne Carroll
Boone Creek Hospital - Kristi Hombs Kopydlowski
Nurse Rae Anne - Kim Kurtz
Shelley Jasper - Belinda Jackson Hercule
Dante Columbe - April Shindlebower Brown
Whiskey Slinger's - Dana Hiser - Chapter 8, 10
The Bourbon House - Karen Cranford LeBeau
Travis Preston - Ginna Honeycutt
Tito Hogan - Karen Cranford LeBeau
Riverside bar - Jo West
Oakleigh Montgomery - Jana Wells

A special thank you to Judy Rosen, my amazing editor!

Last but not least, my family for the love and sacrifices they have made and continue to make to help me achieve this dream, especially my husband and best friend, Gene. Words can never express how much you mean to me.

To our veterans and current serving members of our armed forces, police and fire departments, thank you ladies and gentlemen for your hard work and sacrifices; it's with gratitude and thankfulness that I mention you in this forward.

DESCRIPTION

A RAPTOR operative who wants revenge.

A doctor who has vowed to first do no harm.

The ultimate clash of what they both believe in.

Emersyn Copeland has been on the hunt for the man who betrayed all she had been trained to do. So close to capturing him, she'll stop at nothing, even when her ability to walk is at stake. When her body gives out, she is compelled to turn to the one man who brings her a glimmer of hope in terms of walking without pain again.

Chase Nicholas was trained as a doctor in the Army. He was selected to become part of a special medical unit established to develop drugs and prosthetics to enhance wounded soldiers' abilities and create a stronger more powerful Army. It is a matter of pride for him. What he didn't know is that he wasn't the finish line for these drugs, there was a special team taking his work and producing something more powerful. Accidentally using it on Emmy changes both of their worlds forever.

Will the military stop Chase before he can reengage both Emersyn's trust and her heart?

Let's stay in touch where bots, algorithms and subjective admins don't decide what we see. PJ Fiala's Readers' Club is my newsletter where I promise to only send you content you enjoy! https://www.subscribepage.com/pjfialafm

1

Emmy crept along the edge of the road where it met up with the land surrounding the house they believed Anton Smith was living in. Or was it hiding in? Either way, it didn't at all look like a home a billionaire would be caught dead in. She grinned as she thought about Smith being dead. Then realized she wanted him very much alive. He deserved the punishment he was about to receive, and he needed to be alive to live through it. If only she could see him every day in jail and watch his deterioration unfold.

Diego and Falcon had entered the dense woods in front of the house about a half hour ago. She was told to stay back because of the uneven footing in the woods and she'd just recently recovered from a locked hip. Her nose scrunched when she thought about what was happening to her body. She was only twenty-eight and she was facing life in a wheelchair very soon. She'd always been so active and running was her jam. That all stopped the day her MRAP hit an IED and she'd shattered her hip.

She shook her head and limped along the perimeter of the woods, not hearing a sound except the cicadas, frogs, birds, and squirrels. Of course, they made so much noise it was impossible to hear anything else. Hopefully, it was that way for Diego and Falcon.

She had her comm unit on, and so did they, but sometimes it was easy to hear their voices when the world was listening. No doubt, Smith would be listening. Especially if he thought they were on to him.

Emmy ventured further along the road, looking at her phone and the map on it for direction. The road she walked turned and meandered along the bottom of this hill for what seemed like miles. The oppressive heat caused a river of sweat to trickle down her back and between her breasts and the myriad of bugs dive-bombing her head made her miss home.

A hissing sound stopped her forward motion, which jarred her right hip. Slowly looking for the culprit, a coiled copperhead snake rose its head and stared at her.

She took a deep breath and slowly walked backward, keeping her eye on the snake. She'd happily shoot it if it wouldn't stir up attention. Sadly, that's exactly what it would do.

Her comm unit clicked, "Em, I have a visual on the house. I don't see anyone stirring and it looks like a dump. There's old furniture, buckets, and garbage all over the porch. I don't think the front door is used at all, there's no path to get to it." Diego reported.

She replied, "It's probably full of snakes too."

Falcon then commented. "I have a visual on the side of the house facing the south. There's a back door and a garage back here."

Shots rang out and she had trouble figuring out if they were from her comm unit or close to her. Her question was answered when a bullet whizzed above her head and hit the tree across the road. Turning quickly, she began jogging, which was only half-jogging half-hopping on her good leg to get back to the SUV.

"I'm spotted." She reported.

Falcon's voice sounded breathless as he said, "Me too. Get to the SUV."

Diego replied, "On it."

Their labored breathing sounded in unison as they each ran to their SUV. Emmy saw something out of the corner of her eye and turned to see who or what it was. Twisting her right hip, she cried out in pain as she fell to the ground.

The hot pavement scratched and burned her skin as the pain seared through her hip and down her leg causing her to become dizzy and nauseous. She grunted as she tried taking breaths, each small movement felt like a hot knife sliding into her hip.

"Emmy!" Falcon ran to her and knelt down.

"I can't move."

Diego reached them under another round of gunshots and ducked behind the SUV. Falcon heaved out a deep breath. "This is gonna hurt and I'm sorry."

He stood, then knelt down and scooped her up in his arms. She cried out in pain as he laid her in the very back of the SUV then climbed in with her.

Things were happening around her, though the pain made her float in and out of consciousness. She could feel the vehicle as it turned corners and sped down the road. She kept her eyes closed because her mind couldn't take in anything else.

"Em, tell me what you feel."

As she opened her mouth, a wave of nausea rolled up her belly and she clapped her hand over her mouth.

"Shit."

Falcon scrambled around a bit in the back of the SUV, though he was careful and didn't jostle her at all, which she was grateful for.

He was at her side in a moment as she swallowed numerous times and tried taking a deep breath.

"Em, I'm going to lift your head slightly and put a bottle of water at your lips. You need to sip a bit of water."

"K."

Falcon's hand slid behind her head and he carefully lifted her up. She felt the bottle of water at her lips and sipped as the cold liquid touched her lips. He pulled the water back for a few seconds, then touched her lips with the bottle once again. "Just a sip."

She sipped lightly and he gently laid her head down. The SUV turned and slowed, she inhaled deeply and opened her eyes.

Falcon's concerned eyes were staring at her and she tried to smile, but it felt like a wince.

"Is everyone alright?"

"Everyone except you."

Closing her eyes, she nodded until she felt the SUV turn and hit a bump. She groaned and Falcon stretched out next to her on her left side, at least as much as he could.

"I'll sit tightly to you, which will hopefully ease the movement of the vehicle until we get to the hospital."

"I don't need a hospital."

He chuckled, "God you're so fucking stubborn. You need a hospital, and besides you needing the help, there's no fucking way I'm going back to that house and telling my wife I didn't take you to the hospital."

"Chicken."

"Yes. Deal with it."

"Did you call Kori?"

"Yes. She'll meet us at the hospital in Boone Creek."

She swallowed and nodded before letting her eyes close. The vehicle came to an abrupt stop and a flurry of activity swirled around her.

The hatch opened and Falcon slid from beside her and a chorus of voices she didn't know started shouting out questions.

"What is her injury?"

"She has a bad hip, it was decimated in an IED explosion in Afghanistan about five years ago."

"What caused her to injure it today?"

"She was running from gunfire and injured it."

"Who was shooting at her?"

"I don't know."

"What's her name?"

"Emersyn Copeland."

A female voice called out to her. "Emersyn, can you hear me?"

She raised her hand and nodded.

"On a scale of 1 being no pain and ten being maximum pain, what is your pain level?"

"Fifteen."

"Okay dear, we'll help you with that shortly."

The sound of wheels could be heard, then voices talking outside of the vehicle again.

Falcon's voice reached her. "Em. I'm sorry, but I'm going to pick you up and lay you on a stretcher. It's gonna hurt, but I'll try to be fast."

She swallowed and took a deep breath. She felt his hands slide under her torso and then under her knees. She took a deep breath and tried to hold it, but the instant he picked her up, she yelled out. That was the last thing she felt.

2

Chase trotted down the hall, Nurse Rae Anne running with him.

"What is her pain level?"

"She said fifteen."

"Oh boy. And the extent of her injury today?"

"Her hip is purple and swollen and it looks as though there are multiple bone fractures based on the lumps visible under the skin. The X-rays are developing now."

"Okay. What's her age?"

"Twenty-eight."

He shook his head. "I'll grab the X-rays while you get her into the emergency room and prepped."

He hurried to the X-ray technician's office, dodging nurses and patients in the corridors.

Entering the X-ray tech's office, he was greeted with a furrowed brow and a slow shake of Dante Columbe's head.

"It's not good, Chase."

"Let me see."

Dante handed him the packet of X-rays he held and Chase moved them over to the lightbox to his left on the wall.

He tucked each X-ray into the metal clips and turned on the light. What he saw made his tummy flip.

"Wow," he murmured. "This poor woman must be in extraordinary pain."

"Yes. That's what I said when I first looked at them. I've managed to count twenty-two fractures at the head of the femur. I can't imagine packing her femur with cement would work in this case, she doesn't have enough bone structure to mend together."

Chase nodded his head. "It looks as though there are fractures in the socket also."

He studied the X-rays and mentally grabbed for what he'd say to his patient. She was young, too young to be confined to a wheelchair for the remainder of her life if something could help her.

He heaved out a deep breath and turned toward the door. "I'll pop back in here after I examine her."

"I'll keep them up on the lightbox."

Chase exited the room and moved down the corridor to the emergency patient rooms. Entering the emergency wing of the hospital, Nurse Rae Anne, met him at the door.

"She's in room six. Her pain level hasn't subsided."

"Thanks, Rae Anne."

He pulled a pair of gloves from the holder on the wall and quickly tugged them on his hands. Using his elbow, he slid the glass door open. His patient, Emersyn Copeland, lay on the bed in the room, her face contorted in pain. Another woman sat in a chair next to the bed, holding Emersyn's hand. He swallowed the enormous lump in his throat as he once again read her name. Emersyn.

He nodded to the woman sitting next to the bed, then turned to Emersyn. Nurse Rae Anne stepped in behind him and closed the door. His head then swiveled back to the woman sitting in the chair.

"Kori?"

Her eyes rounded and she stood. "Chase?" She took a step toward him, "I didn't know you worked here. I thought you worked at a hospital outside of Fort Leonard Wood."

"This is outside of Fort Leonard Wood. I didn't expect to see you here."

"I left you a voicemail but didn't hear back."

Chase's cheeks heated slightly. "I've been pulling double shifts here. Sorry."

Kori turned to Emersyn, "Emmy, this is Chase Nicholas. The doctor I told you about."

He nodded at Kori then turned to Emersyn. The second their eyes locked he recognized her. He'd never forgotten those deep brown eyes and her full lips. He'd dreamt about those soft lips.

"Emersyn?"

Surprise was evident by the rounding of her eyes. She grimaced as she adjusted herself in the bed, but her eyes locked on his once again, and she stared.

"Chase. I didn't expect to ever see you again."

Kori turned her head to and fro between them. Finally, she looked at Emmy, her brows furrowed, "You mean you know him?"

"Yes."

Kori turned to him, her expression unreadable. "You know her?"

He looked into Emmy's eyes once again and his cheeks heated. He remembered how her lips felt against his. How her body felt pressed to him. He remembered...

"How do you two know each other?" Kori demanded.

Emmy gasped and both he and Kori turned their attention to her.

"Emmy, I need to see your hip."

"No, we should just go. I..." She gasped once again as she moved her legs.

Rae Anne rushed to her bedside and laid her left hand on Emmy's shoulder. "Emersyn, you need to lay still so the pain isn't so great until we can get you pain meds."

"I'll go somewhere else."

"No, you're here now and to go somewhere else would take time, energy you don't have, and it will be painful. Let Dr. Nicholas help you."

Emersyn lay back with a whoosh of air from her lungs and closed her eyes.

He felt bad right now. It was because of him that she didn't want to stay for the treatment she so clearly needed.

"Emmy." He watched her eyes open and focus on him. Stepping closer to the right side of her bed, he calmly said, "I'm an orthopedic specialist here at Boone Creek Hospital. I've been one for a few years now and I'm very good. I've worked with countless military personnel over the years both on base and here. I'm not trying to brag, but military injuries are my specialty and..." He lightly cleared his throat. "I'm very good at what I do."

She bit her bottom lip, her eyes locked on his and if he wasn't in doctor mode right now, it would have been much harder not to bend down and kiss her lips.

He waited for her to agree and felt a huge weight of relief when she finally agreed with a shallow nod.

Taking the two steps to stand before her injured hip, he gently lifted the sheet careful not to expose too much of her body. He nodded to reassure her, then glanced down at her injury. Small scars, now somewhat faded, revealed themselves to his eyes. He ran his finger along the scars to see if he could feel cording in them. Her hip was purple and swollen. Emersyn gasped in pain at his light touch.

"I see you've had surgeries on your hip."

"Yes."

"Are you aware of what those surgeries consisted of? I don't have benefit of your medical records just yet."

Emersyn shifted ever so lightly on the bed, her lips pulled into a thin line. She let out a deep breath once she'd finished moving. "The first one was to see if they could do anything." She pointed to the scar. "The second one was to remove some cartilage that had broken off and was piercing a nerve. The third one was to remove some pieces of bone that had broken away."

"Okay. What hospital did you have these surgeries performed in? Rae Ann will get them ordered."

"Walter Reed Medical Hospital."

His eyes shot to Kori's then back to Emersyn. "You had surgery at Walter Reed and they weren't able to help you?"

"Right."

"How long ago was this?"

"Five years." The effort she expended talking to him was evident.

He took a deep breath. "I'll order some pain meds for you now while I figure out what we can do for you. I'm sure you're aware your hip is shattered. The femur looks like a tattered flag at this point and conventional medicine and surgeries will do you no good."

Her deep brown eyes looked deeply into his and he found himself compelled to stare. "I have a mission to complete. We're so close and we can't let him get away. Whatever you can do to help me get back to the field, please do it."

His heart pounded in his chest. "Let me get some pain meds for you and re-examine your X-rays."

He stepped back and turned to Rae Anne. "Let's start her on Vicodin and monitor where her pain levels drop while she's here. I'll enter the order. Set up an IV of Toradol."

Emersyn yelled out, "No." She swallowed and lowered her voice. "No IV. I need to get out of here."

Raye Anne looked at him and waited. He inhaled deeply and nodded slightly. "Just the Vicodin for now."

"Sounds good."

"Emersyn, I'll be back soon."

He turned to leave, and Kori stopped him. "Chase, I'd like to chat with you now if possible."

His eyes dropped to Emersyn's. His mind raced around Kori's connection with her.

Emersyn closed her eyes a moment, then looked at Kori. "Nothing about me."

It was a statement not a question and through her pain, Emersyn conveyed a certain authority.

"I promise."

"And I need to get out of here soon."

Emersyn closed her eyes and Kori frowned before glancing at him once again and tilting her head toward the door.

3

The pain meds helped. As long as she was perfectly still, she could manage to think and talk without feeling like her leg was being cut off by a saw. Probably a bit over the top, but that was the best description she could come up with at the moment.

She raised her head up higher in the mechanical bed and looked at her phone. No one had sent any information to her.

She pulled up a fresh text to all of her team members. "I won't be here long. Kori is talking with my doctor now and as soon as they return, I'll be released. In the meantime, pull up the real estate records on that house we found. See if there is anything associated with it in the local newspapers too. That is not a house Anton Smith would live in."

She tapped send then pulled up the RAPTOR system on her phone. She found the notes on this mission and grinned as she read a message from Deacon. "Anton Sylvester Smith. His initials are ASS. It's perfect."

Other team members were making rude comments and she enjoyed reading them. It took her mind off her current dilemma. What in the hell would she do if she couldn't ever walk again? She had money now and between her and her family's connections in the world at large, it was a real possibility that someone would be able to invent or create a prosthetic that would strap around her waist and help her to walk. That would absolutely be a route she'd consider. And, in all the hospitals in the world, how was it that she came to this one to see none other than Chase Nicholas?

He'd hurt her so bad. She'd vowed never to get involved with anyone in her same line of work because of him. But, sadly, not only had that been her mandate from that point forward, but it also kept her from dating anyone. She was busy building a business and she didn't have time to date. But just the thought of dating anyone made her think of him, and she just couldn't do it. Wouldn't do it...maybe.

Her phone chimed and she read a text from Falcon. "Where is Kori now?"

"Talking with Dr. Nicholas."

Falcon was head over heels for Kori. She enjoyed watching him change as he found her and fell in love. He was still a bit broody at times, but when Kori was around, it was far less.

The door to her room slid open and Falcon and Diego stepped inside.

"Hey."

Falcon responded first. "Hey. So, what did he say?"

"You mean Dr. Nicholas?"

Falcon ran his palms over his knees as he sat in the chair Kori recently vacated. "Yeah."

"My femur looks like a tattered flag. No possibility for surgery. He's assessing my options."

Even as she said it a heavy weight pressed down on her chest. Tears threatened to spill, and she clenched her jaw together to stop the flow of tears. She. Didn't. Cry.

Diego sat in the second chair in the room and took a deep breath. "Fuck I hate hospitals."

She huffed out a breath. "Me too."

Diego leaned forward and laid his elbows on his knees. "We'll finish this mission and stop Anton Smith, Em. No matter what, we're ready, willing, and able. You know that. You have to focus on not permanently altering your life for the worse."

She squirmed in her bed and adjusted herself, pleased that it didn't hurt as much as it had. "Getting Anton Smith off the streets and making sure he never sees the light of day again, is worth anything that happens to me."

Falcon shook his head, "Do not let Anton Smith change your life. It is us who will change his."

Her door opened and Kori and Dr. Nicholas stepped inside. Kori smiled at Falcon, then walked to him.

"Falcon, this is my friend, Dr. Chase Nicholas. Chase, this is my husband, Falcon Montgomery."

Chase stepped further into the room and held his hand out to shake Falcon's. Falcon stood and shook hands with Chase then sat down once again and pulled Kori down on his lap. Emmy grinned and glanced at Diego to see him grinning as well.

Dr. Nicholas looked into her eyes and she thought how attractive his features were. He was different in that he wasn't a rugged-looking man. That's sort of what she was used to. He was clean-shaven. His eyes were light brown and he had nice eyelashes. Her eyes landed on his hands that held a tablet close to his chest; they were clean and smooth looking. But not like her hands. His were larger, strong, and steady.

He took a deep breath and addressed her. "Emmy."

"Emersyn."

He stopped briefly, then nodded, "Emersyn. I understand you want to leave today and not be admitted."

"That's correct. I have to finish my mission."

"Do you understand that any wrong move at this point will permanently destroy your hip? We might be able to add fillers to the fractures and see if we can mend them. But if you continue to injure your hip, fragments of those frail bones will break off and we'll not be able to repair..."

"Chase. You can help her."

His eyes darted to Kori and he took a deep breath, but she interrupted.

"Chase, you have to do this."

He shook his head, "Kori. I can't..." He looked around the room. "Not now. I've explained my situation."

Emmy sat higher in her bed. "You two need to fight it out later. I need to finish my job and we're wasting valuable time. Smith knows someone was lurking around that house. I'd bet my good hip they've run the plates and are likely at the rental store right now finding out who we are. We. Don't. Have. Time."

Kori turned to her. "You don't understand. He..."

Emmy held her hand up to stop Kori from continuing. "I don't know what you think he can do for me, but I cannot let Anton Smith go. He has to be stopped before he can pull his operation back together."

She pulled the sheet around her tighter and struggled to turn and dangle her feet over the bed. "Unless you all want to see what my momma gave me, you better get out of here so I can get dressed."

"Emersyn, please don't make any rash movements." Chase begged.

Falcon and Diego stood and nodded, then made a beeline for the door. Kori nodded to Falcon, and he scowled at Dr. Nicholas before ducking out with Diego.

"You don't understand Dr. Nicholas..."

"Chase. Please, call me Chase." He inhaled a deep breath, "Before you say more, I'd like to know what it is that is so important for you to risk your ability to walk."

4

He waited patiently for her to say something. Anything. He'd likely heard it all before. Young girls or women, usually high school and college age, always said the same thing. 'Volleyball is everything. If I don't get a scholarship I won't get into - name the college.' Or, 'It's my last year to play softball, I have to play.' The reasons, while important to them, didn't seem to be equal, at least in his mind, to the fact that they'd live the rest of their lives with this injury that would cause them so much pain later on.

Emersyn adjusted herself in the bed and blew his mind. "We save trafficked women and children. That's what we are. Actually, it's who we are. We are in the final stages of capturing the kingpin of a large operation that has been in the business of trafficking for years. Years. Do you know how many women and children have lost their lives to these assholes? Thousands. I won't stop working until Anton Smith has been brought to justice or is dead. That's what's so important."

Chase swallowed. His vision darkened to a point he struggled to see because everything was blackening in front of him. Fade to dark was a real thing. He swallowed and blinked a few times and Kori touched his arm. "Chase, are you alright?"

He blinked again and Kori came into focus. She pulled him to a chair and pushed him gently to sit. He took a few deep breaths, then looked up to find Emersyn staring at him, her head cocked to the left slightly.

Turning his head to Kori at his right, he tried to smile but it felt forced. "I'm fine. Truly."

"You're pale as a ghost Chase. What on earth just happened?"

He took a deep breath and let it out slowly. "I just...Nothing. I'm fine. I guess I just felt light-headed. I didn't eat today."

"A doctor should know better." Kori admonished.

He stood slowly but didn't take a step. "You're right about that. We've been working double shifts and I've been running from patient to patient. It's simply bad judgment on my part not to have brought a lunch today."

Kori pulled her phone out and tapped out a text then looked at Emersyn. "Emmy, can we at least talk with Chase about some alternatives for you to accomplish what you need to do in your mission and still not completely destroy your ability to walk again?"

His mind still reeled from Emersyn's reasoning for not listening to him in terms of taking it easy until she could heal. Nicola. His sweet little sister Nicola. He thought about her often but more often when he was home with his parents. When he was mind-numbingly busy, he managed to put her to the back recesses of his mind.

Emersyn looked into Kori's eyes and her face softened. She was still pretty. Dark brown eyes and long dark hair. Emersyn was petite in bone structure, but she wasn't weak. Even now at rest, in the hospital bed across from him, her bottom half was covered in a sheet, but her upper body encased in a black tank top, and her arm muscles were defined. And, physical toughness aside, she was mentally strong.

"Okay. Let's talk about what some of my options might be then." She crossed her arms in front of her. He tried not to chuckle; she was already protecting herself against what she didn't want to hear.

He studied her a moment before speaking. "Do you mind if I step out for just a moment? I'm going to grab a few pamphlets of options for you and I'm afraid I need a drink of water."

What he needed was a moment to clear his head.

Emersyn nodded lightly, and he concentrated on his feet to get him out the door. Taking deep breaths as he strode to his office, he prayed no one would speak to him until he could get a moment of peace.

Gratefully slipping into his office and locking the door behind him, he leaned against the door for a few moments until his mind unlocked itself from the extreme grief that had washed over him. Then he shuffled the few steps to his desk and sat with a thud in his chair.

Taking in the photographs on his desk, his eyes landed on Nicola. She was seven years old and adorable. Her smile was a constant and she loved him as much as he loved her. He and his older brother, Drake, were devastated when she was taken. Her body had been found four years later. Police felt she'd been trafficked and thrown away. His family reeled from the horror of it all. Years later he joined the Army and then trained as a doctor. When he'd met Kori years later, he helped her free of charge as a way to make his sister's death mean something more than just a little girl gone. Some of the women Kori helped, he thought could have been Nicola. He'd hoped on more than one occasion that maybe, just maybe she was still alive and through happenstance, he'd find her. Maybe they'd buried the wrong girl.

He stared at Nicola's smiling face for a few more moments and made up his mind. He'd help her. He would find a way to help Emersyn put men like this Anton Smith away.

He picked up the phone and dialed the number that would change his life forever. He'd find it easy to forgive himself and, if in the end, he lost his medical license, so be it. He'd do it for Nicola. He'd help Emersyn for Nicola.

"Hello."

"Hey, it's Chase Nicholas. I need a favor."

5

Emmy waited in the emergency room with Kori. Falcon entered with a bag of food and it smelled both heavenly and then, not. Her stomach roiled and she closed her eyes.

Kori jumped up and touched her left shoulder. "Em. Are you alright?"

She inhaled slowly and waited before letting the air from her lungs. "Yes. The smell of the food initially made me nauseous, but it seems to have passed."

"You haven't had food today either. I asked Falcon to bring you and Chase something to eat."

"What about you three? You haven't eaten either."

Kori looked at Falcon and he shrugged. "Well, actually we did. We ate in the waiting area because I was starving."

She glanced at Falcon's sheepish grin and smiled at him in return. "I'm glad you ate. We need to keep all of you healthy."

The door opened and Chase stepped in. His nose wrinkled briefly, and Falcon held out the bag to him, kissed Kori's lips, then he ducked out of the room.

Chase looked at the bag then at her. Emmy shrugged. "Kori ordered us food."

Kori took the bag from Chase and pulled the rolling tray to her bedside, then pulled food from the bag. "You two need to eat. If Emmy has take Vicodin, she's going to need something on her tummy. You can't run around here all light-headed and be good at your job if you aren't healthy. So..." She turned and pulled a chair from against the wall and slid it on the other side of the rolling tray. "Sit and eat and tell us what you can do for Em."

Emmy watched Chase obey Kori's orders and sit. He immediately pulled a burger from the tray and laid it in his lap. As he unwrapped the burger he asked, "May I eat first?"

Kori laughed. "Yes. Please eat. Em, you need to eat too."

She tested the strength of her stomach by inhaling once again and when the aroma of the burger and fries before her didn't make her want to vomit, she slowly reached for the remaining burger on the tray and set it in her lap. The door slid open once again and Falcon entered the room with two bottles of water. "I thought you'd like something to drink, so..." He shrugged and set the water on the tray.

Kori smiled at her husband. "Thanks, Babe. That's very thoughtful of you."

Falcon kind of groaned but his cheeks deepened in color and he smiled at his wife, then quickly ducked out again.

It was cute. She'd never tell Falcon that, he'd likely go off on a tangent if he thought anyone thought he was cute.

She smiled at Kori, who smiled widely in return and her cheeks turned an adorable shade of pink as well.

Chase inhaled his burger, then reached for the water and unscrewed the cap. Instead of taking a drink, he set that one on her side of the rolling tray and grabbed the other water bottle, and opened that one for himself. Now it was her turn for pink cheeks. But it was stupid.

He then used one of the napkins on the tray and wiped his lips. She found herself unable to stop watching him. Her brain was likely drug-addled at this moment from the Vicodin, but she didn't want to be attracted to Chase Nicholas ever again. Now, she felt a bit self-conscious because he'd seen her scars. He knew what a damaged mess she was. And, he was likely married by now. He'd told her all those years ago that he was engaged.

Chase stood and dropped his napkin into the wastebasket. "Kori that was kind of you and Falcon to bring me lunch. It was unnecessary, but I thank you just the same." He turned toward her then glanced again at Kori. "Also, we're not supposed to eat in here, so when Rae Anne comes back in, I did not eat here."

"You're welcome. You both needed to eat. And, got it."

Chase inhaled deeply. Standing at the sink, he washed his hands, then pulled toweling from the holder on the wall. Drying his hands, he then tossed the wadded paper toweling into a wastebasket. "Okay. So, what I'm about to tell you needs to be kept confidential. You can't ever go public with this, and you need to keep it within this room.

Kori, I know you'll say you want to tell Falcon and I'll say this, you may tell him, but that's where it ends. I'd never want someone to hold a secret from their spouse."

Emmy closed her eyes and bit the inside of her cheek so she didn't scoff loudly at that statement.

"Chase, I won't tell anyone except Falcon."

Chase turned and stared into her eyes and she found them mesmerizing. The same hazel eyes rimmed with thick lashes, he was still incredibly handsome.

"I promise to keep this between us."

"Emersyn, I don't know if you're married or have a significant other, so let me say that..."

She halted him first with her hand held up in the air, palm toward him. "I'm not married, and I don't have a significant other."

His cheeks warmed and he nodded. "Okay, then let me say this. While I was in the Army, I worked on a special project named, Superman. We were tasked with creating a serum to help soldiers and Marines heal faster so they could return to the battlefield sooner. I guess it was in some ways mad science, but I loved the idea behind it."

Emmy watched his eyes dart to the door then back to her and Kori.

"I'm not allowed to use this serum on civilians. I still have clearance to use it when necessary on base, but not outside of it."

His cheeks deepened now and it looked good on him. "I honestly believe it's the only way to help you, Emmy.

Emersyn. The condition of your femur negates all other available treatments."

She nodded and bit her bottom lip. "I understand."

Chase sat in the chair again and pushed the rolling tray to the wall. "I'm not sure you do. There'll be no guarantees. There'll be no recourse if it doesn't work. There'll be no way to reverse it. Basically, you'll have to agree to a totally experimental procedure with no form of rebuke should it not work."

She swallowed. Really, what choice did she have? It was either try something like this or be in a wheelchair. In a wheelchair, she'd have to change how she performed her job. She'd likely not be able to go on missions. How effective would she be at leading a team when she couldn't do the work?

But still, she didn't want to be rash. "Can I think about it?"

"Of course. I encourage you to as a matter-of-fact. This isn't something you should decide on the spur-of-the-moment."

She inhaled a deep breath and glanced at Kori. "What do you think?"

Kori shook her head slowly. "It's not my decision..."

"I'm asking. If it were you or Falcon, what would you do?"

Kori's shoulders dropped. "I'd do it." She tucked a long lock of hair behind her ear. "But I'd ask all the questions first."

"Such as."

"Such as how long does it take? Is it painful? How many others have used this and what happened to them? Among others."

"Fair enough."

"And the final question. Why? Why is he trusting you?"

6

Chase stared at Kori. Her eyes refused to look into his and he knew it was because she felt sheepish for her last question. But she was right.

He took a deep breath and turned to face Emersyn. The beautiful, vivacious, stunning, badass woman who he had to help.

And she asked it. "Why?"

He blinked and locked eyes with Emersyn. She repeated herself. "Why? It's the best question, so I'm asking it first."

He took a deep breath and closed his eyes. "I trust you. I know you. The job you're all doing requires a huge amount of secrecy, planning, and diligence. So..." He shrugged. "I trust you not to say anything."

"But there's something else. I can tell by the way you're hesitating."

He stood and paced to the door, turned, and paced toward her. "I have a personal reason."

"What's your personal reason?"

She looked at him, not blinking and it caused his heartbeat to increase. He cleared his throat lightly. He glanced briefly at Kori, who sat transfixed as she waited for him to respond. He hadn't told her about Nicola. He didn't tell anyone about her.

He rubbed the back of his neck with the fingers of his right hand, and he practiced steadying his breathing. His fingers shook. He pulled his hand down and slid it into his trouser pocket.

Opening his mouth he hesitated. Closing his mouth when words wouldn't come, he closed his eyes.

"I have a personal reason."

Emersyn inhaled deeply and loudly. "Your wife? Is that your personal reason?"

"No."

Kori leaned forward. "Chase, you didn't tell me you got married."

"I didn't."

His eyes darted to Emersyn then back to Kori. Kori's brows furrowed and she turned to Emersyn.

"Em, I feel like I'm missing some part of a story here."

"Yes, you are. Chase, would you like to tell her?"

His chest hurt from the pounding of his heart and the look in Emersyn's eyes. The hurt on her face took his breath away.

"I didn't get married."

"Why not? You ended things with me because you said you were engaged."

"I didn't get married."

Emersyn shook her head and her brows rose in her hairline. "So you lied?"

"No, I didn't lie. I was engaged. At the time. But, after you..."

"Oh my God. Please don't say you couldn't go through with it and you ended your engagement. I mean, seriously, Chase. Grow a spine."

Emersyn twisted in the bed and dangled her feet over the side. Her face pinched as he assumed the pain seared through her body.

"Emersyn, please don't do yourself harm."

She held her hand up to stop his speaking and he froze and waited for her.

Kori took a deep breath, "I think I need to leave you two alone for a bit."

"No!" Emersyn yelled. She shook her head and swallowed then took a deep breath. "I'm sorry Kori. I didn't mean to yell. I need help getting dressed and getting out of here. If all I can do is use crutches, or worst-case scenario, a wheelchair, then so be it, but I won't stay here any longer and I don't want to talk about this bullshit with Chase anymore."

His mind went back to doctor mode. "Emmy." She glared. "Emersyn. Please. We don't have to talk about this anymore, but please don't do anything to hurt yourself further."

Her eyes landed on his. "Well, then, Doctor Nicholas. Can I walk?"

"With great discomfort."

"Which I've been doing for years."

"You have to be incredibly careful. When turning you need to rely on your left leg and only pivot or change direction with your left leg leading."

"I've been doing that for years also."

"Please. Stay here and let me help you."

Her head hung down as it appeared as though she was studying her feet. She tested the movement in her right leg by first flexing and squeezing her toes. She moved to rotate her ankle. Then lifting her leg at the knee, then slowly letting it down. Her face pinched here and there as she made the movements, which told him she still had pain. That might not be the worst thing, she would take a bit of care if she intended to leave the hospital.

"It appears I can move my leg and toes."

"But you shouldn't bear weight on your right leg."

"Then I'll use crutches. I can sit for much of my job. I don't have to be completely in the field but direct from the sidelines. I can still use a gun if need be."

"But if you can't run, you'll be putting yourself in danger and could get yourself killed."

Kori then stood, "Or someone else."

The two women stared at each other for a long time. No words were spoken but silent messages were conveyed. Finally, Emmy said, "I will never put my team at risk for my own gain."

A tear slid down Kori's cheek and Chase swallowed the emotion in his throat. He'd seen Kori through all sorts of tough issues with the women she'd rescued but he'd never seen her cry.

"I can't lose Falcon because of your pride."

"If you lose Falcon, it will never be because of me or my pride."

"I'm going to make you keep your word on that. What you all do is dangerous enough. Don't make it more so."

Emmy swallowed then turned her beautiful face to him. "I'll need crutches and a prescription for Vicodin."

His shoulders fell forward as he let her words sink in. She was stubborn. He knew that. He knew she would see things through with this mission before she ever put herself first and he'd need to find a way to make sure she did come back to him for help. And he wanted the opportunity to set things right with her. He'd left things a terrible mess. He tried to set them right with her, but he had been too late. She'd already gone.

7

Oh, those stupid emotions that flooded her head. Her heart. Her body. Ugh!

Her feet still hung over the side of her bed and Kori knelt before her to help with her pants. The throbbing was suppressed for now and the aching that ran down her leg was now minimal.

"Okay Em, put your left foot into the leg of your pants first. Then, I'll scrunch them up and slide your right foot into the other leg."

She inserted her right foot into her pants leg and Kori pulled the bottom of her pant leg up over her foot. Scrunching up the left pant leg, she held the leg hole open and Emmy pointed her toe and Kori slipped her pant leg over her foot. Kori pulled her pants up to her knees and made sure the bottom of her pants was pushed up over her foot so she wouldn't trip.

Kori stood and pulled one of the chairs over to her right side, the back of the chair facing her.

Kori positioned herself at her side. "Push off the bed and if you need help, I'll support you under your arm."

"Okay. The Vicodin has helped. If the swelling would go down that would sure help too."

Kori nodded. "We can put you on ice when we get to the house. We'll control your diet too. No salty foods for a while."

Emmy wrinkled her nose. "Sounds boring and bland."

"It's temporary."

"Yeah."

Kori positioned herself in front of her. "Hands on my shoulders, not around my neck. And if you don't feel you need me and can push off the bed yourself, I'll support you under your arms."

Emmy nodded, tightened her butt muscles while pushing forward off the bed, and used the chair to support herself. Her left foot touched the floor first, then her right foot, but she held herself to the left keeping her weight distribution to one side.

Her left foot touched the floor first, then her right foot, but she held herself to the left keeping her weight distribution to one side.

She reached out with her right hand and grabbed the back of the chair.

Kori loosened her grip and looked into her eyes. They were fairly similar in height and weight and both of them were dark-eyed and had dark hair. Emmy grinned. "We could be sisters."

Kori smiled. "We are. The family we choose, not the one we have."

She caught the catch in her throat and nodded. "Yep." She whispered because she was trying not to cry. The Vicodin was making her soft and emotional. She needed to get away from Chase Nicholas and this emotional roller-coaster she was riding.

"Are you steady?"

"Yeah."

Kori took a slow step backwards, then another, and stared at her.

Emmy nodded. "It's good."

Kori knelt down and began pulling Emmy's slacks up her legs. When she reached her hips, she stopped and stood.

"Okay, use the chair to steady yourself, but you need to pull your pants up over your hips."

Swallowing the large lump in her throat, she tested her steadiness by letting go of the chairback. Kori stood before her, with her hands out, just in case. Emmy slowly tugged her slacks over her hips, pleased that her right hip didn't hurt like she thought it might. Most of the pain was on the inside.

She zipped and buttoned her slacks and let out a deep breath. "Whew, that wasn't bad."

A slight twinge pulled at her right hip, but she'd had so much worse. She tested a step using her right leg first, clinging to the back of the chair.

She slid her foot out in front of her a slight amount then took a step. Her hip felt like a vise was squeezing it when she stepped, but it was bearable. Which was better than she'd hoped. She tried once again, and it was the same.

The door slid open and Chase stepped in and stared at her.

"Emmy you need to be..."

"Emersyn." She snapped more than she'd intended but she was still mad. Hurt actually.

He huffed out a breath and held out the pair of crutches he held. "My orders are going to include you keeping these with you until you come back for treatment."

She balanced herself on her left foot, then reached forward for the crutches, careful not to touch him.

She tried placing them under her arms, but they were too tall.

Chase knelt down and began adjusting the size for her. She clenched her jaw because she didn't want him doing nice things for her. She needed to keep her heart locked away. He'd already lied to her, or maybe not lied. She didn't know. He told her he was engaged after they'd had a relationship. After they'd spent so much time together. Now, he claimed he didn't get married. How could she ever trust that he was being straight with her?

"Try that now."

She stared at the floor tiles and kept her heart locked up tight. So what, that he was being nice?

"Emmy?"

She turned her head to him. When their eyes met his eyebrows rose into his hairline.

"How does that fit?"

She inhaled deeply, then moved the crutch under her arm. "Good. That fits."

"Okay. It'll only take a few seconds to fit the other one."

He scooted around to her left side and immediately began unscrewing the wing nuts and adjusted the height. Once he'd tightened the nuts, he looked up at her. His eyes were earnest and attractive and sincere and there were fine lines at the corners, and she liked how that looked on him.

"Give it a test and make sure you can manage with them."

She blinked and looked at Kori who stood silently across the room watching her. There'd be questions to answer, she could feel it.

She managed to take the first step and was proud of how smooth it was. Of course, she'd had plenty of practice with crutches, but it had been a little while.

After she'd made a couple more steps, and maneuvered herself back to her bed, Chase pushed the call nurse button on her bed and Rae Anne came into the room a few seconds later.

"How can I help you?" She asked as she entered the room.

"Rae Anne, Emersyn is determined to go home today. I have fitted the crutches for her and I've added a prescription into the computer for her to fill. Please get the details where she wants to pick up her prescription and her care instructions."

"Of course, Dr. Nicholas."

Chase turned to her once again and nodded. "It was nice seeing you again Emersyn." He turned to Kori without waiting for her to respond and she couldn't help but feel she was being dismissed.

"Kori, it was wonderful seeing you again. Next time you're around, how about we find the time to sit and have a drink and really catch up."

"That sounds fantastic Chase. I'll be here for a bit, so Falcon and I will definitely give you a call."

She watched as he left the room without another glance her way and she felt abandoned once again.

8

Chase hurried back to his office before he could change his mind. It was rude. He was rude just now. But she was mad, and he didn't want to get into it. Not now. Plus, as soon as she filled her prescription, she'd likely be mad as hell, and he'd have to deal with that too. But that, he'd handle. He'd give her time, but only two days' worth of time. The eight pills he prescribed wouldn't get her far and she'd be in need again. This gave him time to figure out what he could do and how to do it. And, hopefully, it would give her time to settle down and think logically about it all.

It had been several years now since they'd been together. Not together, together, but he'd taken her out on a few dates. He looked for ways to be around her while they were on base. He'd manufactured reasons to be around her. And he'd kissed her. Touched her. And the whole time he'd been immersed in guilt and remorse. He was engaged to someone else, and it was wrong. Then they made love. Many times. His guilt was enormous, but she was – magnetic.

"Dr. Nicholas?" He swallowed but turned at Rae Anne's call.

"Yes, Rae Anne."

"Did you mean to only prescribe eight pills for Ms. Copeland?"

"Yes."

"But...She'll only get two days out of them for pain relief."

"Yes. And she'll have to come back here. I want the time to offer her some suggestions on how to mend her hip. I was afraid she wouldn't come back here."

Rae Anne's smile slid across her face slowly. Nodding once, she turned and walked back to the nurses' station, and he continued on to his office. Luckily, tomorrow, the new doctor the hospital hired would start work and he'd soon have some time off. The stress of the past few weeks, seeing Emersyn, the lack of sleep, all made his head spin. Nothing seemed right at the moment.

Entering his office, he pulled off his white jacket and hung it in the narrow closet to his right. He pulled the light-weight tan jacket he'd worn in this morning off the hanger and draped it over his arm. Gathering his keys, wallet, and the shopping list he'd made himself this morning, he exited his office and hurried down the corridors to the hospital exit.

The instant he closed the door of his truck, he let out a deeply held breath and willed his body to relax. Taking a few deep breaths, he tapped the "call icon" on his steering wheel and watched the parking lot as his phone engaged.

His truck chimed and he said, "Call Isaac Blair."

The automated voice responded, "Calling Isaac Blair."

Chase started his truck and began moving toward the road. He caught sight of Kori and Falcon helping Emmy into a vehicle and his heartbeat increased. He still had a reaction to her all these years later.

"Hey, hey, hey, what's up with you?"

Isaac's voice interrupted his thoughts, and he huffed out a breath and looked at the road like he should have been doing.

"Hey, man, how are you?"

"I'm good. How about you?"

"Tired. Working doubles."

"That sucks. We're still working the grind here. So, I can't help but think you have something else on your mind, so let's hear it."

Chase's head jerked with the abrupt conversation change then shook. "I guess I can't pull anything over on you. So, I saw Emersyn Copeland today."

"No shit?" Isaac chuckled. "Where?"

"You know I can't say."

"Ah, okay. I get it. So, does she look as hot as she always did?"

Chase swallowed. "Yeah."

"Damn."

"Yeah. So, something's bugging me and I'm hoping you can help me."

"Man, I haven't seen her in years, so if you're asking me to hook you two up, it's a no can do."

"Shut the fuck up. It's not that. But it's also extremely confidential. And violates HIPPA laws and likely a host of others, such as some military confidentiality laws."

Isaac chuckled lightly, then cleared his throat. "Okay, so this is doctor to doctor?"

"Yes." Chase navigated a corner. "And friend to friend."

"Okay."

"Do you have time to meet me?"

"I get off work in an hour. I'm on day shift now."

"Wow, good for you. You're climbing right up the ladder these days."

"Yeah. No. No one climbs right up the ladder in the military man. You know that."

Chase chuckled. "Right." He pulled into a parking space at the grocery store and turned off his truck. "How about we meet at that little bar on Beaver Lake, Whiskey Slinger's."

"You got it. I'll see you there in an hour and a half. It'll take me just a bit to get there."

"I got it. I'll see you there. I'm buying dinner so don't eat."

"You're starting to scare me, Chase."

"Nothing to be scared of. It's just incredibly important for my mental health to talk this all out."

"I'm no counselor, bud."

Chase chuckled. "Not in that way. Something's up and I need someone to help me figure it out. You're the only person I feel safe talking to about this."

He heard Isaac on the other end of the line let out a deep breath. "Okay. See you soon."

The line went dead and he felt slightly better about all the things running through his head. He meant what he said, Isaac would never breathe a word of this to anyone. He was that good of a friend and confidant. There were so few like him in the world.

Heaving himself from his vehicle he sauntered into the grocery store not feeling like doing any of the shopping and once again reminding himself to pay his housekeeper to do it for him. He never saw her, he just knew she'd been there because his house smelled amazing and was neat and tidy. He paid her regularly by scheduled payment apps and it worked for both of them.

His mind then wandered to Emersyn. She likely did her own grocery shopping and enjoyed it. He grinned and shook his head. No, she didn't. She likely was more last minute like him and only ran in when there wasn't anything in the house to eat.

9

Hobbling along on her crutches, she managed quite well under the watchful eye of Kori. There'd be no veering off the path with her close by. Falcon had his hands full if he ever pissed her off. This made her grin, and she was grateful for the millisecond her mind was on something besides her hip, Chase Nicholas, her situation at work, Chase Nicholas, and dammit, Chase Nicholas.

She'd managed over the years to get past the hurt of him leading her on then telling her that it was wrong, and he was engaged. Talk about a sucker punch. He'd never hinted at someone else.

The following day she received her orders to deploy, and she volunteered to leave early with a small readiness group. Her goal was to get far enough away from Chase Nicholas, the cheating bastard, as she could. When she was injured, she blamed that on him too. She shook her head as Falcon opened the door to the SUV.

"What's up?" he asked.

"Nothing. Trying to get out of my own head."

"How's that going?"

She stopped next to the floorboard of the SUV and stood on her left leg while gathering her crutches in her right hand and shoving them at Falcon.

"What do you think?"

He laughed and she used that same anger she'd directed at Chase to pull herself up into the SUV using the overhead handle on the inside of the truck and the armrest.

Grateful her pain was buffered by the Vicodin she slowly adjusted herself in the seat and waited for the others to get in.

Kori sat next to her in the backseat and Falcon and Diego climbed into the front, Diego drove.

"Where to first?" Diego asked.

"I need to get my prescription filled. Then back to the Airbnb so we can plan our next move."

"Gotcha."

Diego carefully maneuvered the SUV out of the parking lot and down the road. Emersyn decided it was time to get her head in the game so she didn't continue to rake Chase Nicholas over the coals in her mind.

"Which pharmacy do you need to go to?"

Kori looked down at the notes and various pamphlets she'd been given and replied, "It's just up the street here. First Street Pharmacy."

"Convenient." He mused.

They pulled into the pharmacy, and he pulled around to the drive-up window. Diego rolled down the window and gave the technician her name.

Emmy closed her eyes and rested her head against the seat back for a moment as that first twinge of pain slid down her leg. Her pain medicine was already beginning to wear off.

Kori softly asked, "Are you beginning to feel pain?"

"Yes."

She nodded then reached forward and touched Falcon's arm. "Babe, we need to get a bag of ice somewhere too."

"Okay. I'll walk across the street to that grocery store and grab a bag." He glanced at Diego who nodded, then exited the vehicle.

She turned her head. "Mixing drinks?"

Kori smiled. "Nope. We're going to ice you down when we get home. It'll help with the swelling. I insist you relax for the rest of the night. They can do some recon work, upload reports, and monitor Smith's whereabouts. You need to rest."

"Kori, we've only been given two weeks to wrap this up."

"I'm aware. I'm also aware that you have built an incredible team of operatives who all want the same thing as you. Let them do their jobs and, for once, think of yourself so you can be part of this. It's huge."

"I know it is." She shook her head and looked out the window of the SUV. The building to her left was pretty. All brick and the flowers outside were incredible. Varying colors of reds, yellows, oranges, and greens were interspersed with pops of white flowers.

She swallowed and half listened as Diego said thank you and handed the small pharmacy bag back to her. She gently leaned forward, feeling the pinch run down her leg. She sucked in her breath and Kori nodded. "Ice."

"What time can I have my next Vicodin?"

Kori looked at her watch and mentally counted the time. "You have another thirty minutes to wait."

Inhaling deeply, Kori reached out her hand for the bag and she reluctantly handed it over, not trusting herself at this moment to follow the schedule. What was a half hour early, anyway?

Kori opened the bag and pulled the bottle from inside. Her brows furrowed and Emmy sat up a bit straighter as she watched her friend examine the contents of the bottle.

Kori's lips formed a straight line as she tucked the bottle into the bag.

"What's wrong with the pills?"

Kori glanced at her and shrugged. "Nothing."

"It doesn't look like nothing."

"It isn't anything really, Em."

"But it's something. So what is it?"

Kori swallowed and her eyes darted to Diego's in the mirror. He drove them across the street to pick up Falcon and she hesitatingly answered.

"Kori! What. Is. It?"

Kori rotated her head then took a deep breath. "There are only eight."

"Eight? Pills? That fucker only gave me eight pills?"

"Em, he must have a good reason for it."

"Oh, I'll bet he has a good reason for it. In his fucked-up mind." Her heart hammered in her chest so hard she thought she'd pass out. How dare he do this to her? He knew she would be in pain for much longer than two days. She'd need something to get her through this mission and then she'd be able to focus on a surgery or serum or whatever, but she needed this mission finished first.

She slammed her fist into the seat in front of her and threw her head back. "That dirty lying cheating fucker."

Kori's head snapped back. "Chase?"

"Yes. Chase. Your 'good' friend." She used air quotes for good.

"He is a good friend. What do you mean cheating, lying..."

"When we were on base together, back in the day. We dated. We were together a lot, but we were taking it slow.

He was always where I was. I fell in love with him." Her eyes darted to Diego's and she didn't care. "Then one day he told me he was engaged to someone else."

"What?"

10

Chase sat at a table in the back of Whiskey Slinger's. The bar was the only bar he ever frequented and by frequented he meant came to about once every two or three months. It was low-key. Quiet. Had an older clientele which he hoped also couldn't hear well and they didn't blare the jukebox or stereo so loud you had to yell to be heard.

He nursed his beer, which tasted amazing, and he gathered his thoughts together before Isaac got there. He stared out the window and wondered at all the time that had passed since he'd last seen Emersyn. Clearly, she'd been involved in an accident and she'd had surgeries but she also mentioned the trafficking she and her co-workers were involved in stopping. Then he thought of Nicola and he knew Emmy and Nic would have loved each other. Emmy was strong. Mentally she was strong. Her family was military, and she'd hinted that her father and grandfather had started a company that did specialty work for the government, but she'd never say more than that. That's likely where she got her strength from. When she spoke of her family it was with pride and admiration. She'd grown up with love and praise and the knowledge that she could be anything she wanted to be. He imagined she worked for her father now.

The door opened and a slice of light filtered in before his friend came into view. Isaac Blair was a tall, proud black man with an easy smile and a brain that was both admirable and enviable. They'd been friends from boot camp on. They went to medical school together and they served together.

He stood as Isaac approached his table and they shook hands and hugged. It had been far too long.

"It's so good to see you man."

Isaac laughed as he hugged him, the vibrations seeping into his body, the warmth of his friend's hug made him feel instantly better.

"It's good to see you too, Chase."

They sat and Chase motioned for the waitress to come over and get his friend a drink.

As she approached, Isaac smiled at her and pointed to him. "I'll have what he's having. Bring two for me and another for my friend."

"You got it."

The waitress, who seemed more interested in what was playing on the television behind the bar than the customers, quickly scooted back to the bar.

Chase looked at his friend. "So, are you going to marry that beautiful woman you've been leading on or not?"

Isaac laughed and the waitress brought their drinks. Isaac tossed two twenties on the table and their waitress quickly made change from her apron then left without a word.

"I'm thinking of popping the question this weekend actually."

Chase laughed. "That's fantastic."

Isaac's smile faded as he looked into Chase's eyes. "But we're here for you. I can see how tired you are. What's going on?"

"I'm tired because I've been working doubles, but we've finally hired another physician and he starts tomorrow, so hopefully my doubles will end soon."

"But that's not why we're here."

Chase used his thumbnail to peel at the label on his beer bottle then took a deep breath.

"No. I'm perplexed to be honest with you."

"Hmm. That doesn't happen often. You're not the kind of man to be perplexed."

Chase swallowed a lump in his throat, then looked up at his friend and stared into his kind, smart, brown eyes.

"Emmy has been injured. She was in an IED explosion in Afghanistan. Her femur is a mess, her hip socket is too, and she's not a candidate for conventional surgery."

"Looks like she came to the right man then. We know you have an ace up your sleeve in that department."

"Well, here's the thing. She was at Walter Reed."

Isaac stopped his bottle halfway to his mouth and froze. Lowering the bottle slowly his brows pinched together. "When?"

"Five years ago."

Both men stared at each other for a long time. "Why didn't they use the serum on her Isaac? They had it there. Doctors at Walter Reed were the ones who told her she wasn't a candidate. SHE and others like her are the reason we created that serum. SHE is the perfect candidate."

Isaac took a long swig from his bottle and set it on the table before him. He looked at his hands for a long time before saying anything. When he did speak, his voice was soft and for his ears only. "I heard rumors."

"What rumors?"

He slowly shook his head. "Keep in mind these are only rumors. I'm not privy to all of the details. I just heard some nurses talking."

"What. Rumors?"

"They weren't using the technology and serums you created in the lab on the military. It went to another facility, and now I've hear they sold it off to others."

"Who? Who would do that?"

Isaac shook his head. "I don't know." His hands motioned to Chase to lower his voice. "I don't know. But I think I can find out."

"I need to know why they wouldn't work on Emmy. Why they wouldn't help her? I need to know what is going on with that serum. I'm attached to it."

"Do you have access now to use it to help Emmy?"

Chase rotated his head. "I made a call today. I'm finding that it's not going to be easy to get my hands on it. But I'm going to do what I have to do to get it."

"And by 'do what you have to do', does that mean illegally?"

"It might be."

Isaac leaned back in his chair and stared at him for a long time. "Chase. Man, don't lose your medical license over this."

"You haven't seen her X-rays. And why wouldn't they help her? How many others are not being helped by the very thing I created for our military personnel?"

"I don't know man. You know, we aren't always in the loop on things. As in, we're seldom in the loop on things."

"Right, but my name is attached to this. I'm listed as one of the creators. Why wasn't I in the loop on this?"

11

Emmy lay on her bed at the Airbnb on her left side. Kori had pillows bunched up behind her and in front of her to keep her in place as she put ice on her right hip. She had a pillow between her legs to keep her hip and leg in line and she was cold.

Kori had given her a Vicodin fifteen minutes early and for a few minutes, she thought she wouldn't be able to relax even with that in her system. But shortly afterward, all trussed up as she was now, she'd succumbed to sleep and managed to rest for about forty-five minutes.

Now though, she was mad again, in pain and trying to keep her mind occupied by scrolling through her computer reading the reports from her operatives, and sorting a plan through her head on their next steps.

A knock sounded at her door and she raised herself up on her elbow as much as she could. "Come in."

The door opened and Creed, Diego, and Falcon stepped inside. "Hey, what's up?"

The three men looked around, then Falcon sat at the foot of the bed, and Creed and Diego sat in chairs opposite her.

Emmy removed the bag of melting ice from her hip, then moved the pillows at her back, and using the strength in her arms, moved herself to a sitting position to rest against the headboard.

Creed answered first. "We've been looking over the reports from Cyber and we're convinced Smith is in that house. It wasn't some hillbilly shooting at us, it was one of Smith's security guards." He tapped his phone and scrolled then turned it toward her and showed her the picture of a man in front of the house they'd been at this afternoon.

"This is Travis Preston, Anton Smith's bodyguard. This is a satellite picture Deacon took about an hour ago." He turned his phone around and tapped a few more times, then turned it to her again. "This is the same man, listed in the payroll records at SmithCo."

"How did you get into SmithCo payroll records?"

Diego laughed, "Piper is a certified hacker. Becca is too."

Falcon added. "They worked together and managed to get into SmithCo's payroll system."

Emmy laughed. "Oh, that's priceless."

Diego nodded. "Also Deacon and Becca are getting married this weekend. Her parents are in Lynyrd Station, and they want to get married while they are still in town. They'll send pictures."

"Oh, that's wonderful. When we finish this mission, we'll have a giant party to celebrate all the weddings we've missed." She motioned to Falcon and his cheeks turned a light shade of pink.

"We'll have to celebrate some babies too." Falcon added.

Emmy cocked her head to the left and looked at him. "Yours?"

"Yeah."

"Congratulations!"

The men fist-bumped each other and Emmy felt warm and fuzzy. Their extended family was growing by leaps and bounds. Diego chuckled, "Charly's pregnant too."

"What? I didn't hear that." Emmy responded.

Diego shrugged. "She told Shelby about fifteen minutes ago. She had to because she's been sick in the morning and Shelby sort of guessed."

Emmy smiled. "Oh, that's so wonderful." Her phone chimed and she looked down at it to see a text from Charly. Giggling, she tapped her message and saw a picture of a positive pregnancy test and the words - "due in seven months. Isabella confirmed it. OMG - I'm going to be a mom."

She turned her phone around so the guys could see it and they chuckled.

Suddenly a sadness fell over Emmy. She pushed it aside to power through this meeting.

"So, I think we go back to the house tonight. We bring scramblers to knock out their cameras. They may suspect we're there, but they won't be able to see where. We need to see what's inside. Bonus if we find Anton Smith. If not him, information as to his whereabouts."

Creed leaned back in his chair. "The funny thing is when we were there today, I didn't see any cars. The garage is in the back, but the door was opened and nothing was in there. That house and a few hundred yards back, and an old barn. It could be they park in the barn, but I don't think they'd allow themselves to be exposed for that long walking to the house. I think there's a secret hiding place somewhere on the grounds."

Falcon nodded. "I think so too. We thought if the three of us go in..."

"Four of us." She corrected.

"Em." Falcon hesitated. "You can't go in. You'll be clumsy on crutches, and you'll be in danger."

She cleared her throat. "I'll sit in the car and keep the scrambler on the cameras. I may also be able to see something from my vantage point that you can't. We'll wear comm units and I'll have several weapons in the SUV with me."

Falcon stared at her, then turned and looked at Diego and Creed.

Creed stood. "I'll agree only if you promise you won't leave the vehicle. Otherwise, you put all of us at risk."

"I'd never do that."

Diego leaned forward, resting his elbows on his knees. "Em. Please think this through."

"I have. I'll be in the SUV and monitoring from there."

Diego nodded slowly then stood. "I'll be ready at dark."

He started to leave the room, but she stopped him. "Diego."

When he turned, she looked him in the eye. "This is the reason RAPTOR exists. We didn't know it was Anton Smith, we only knew about Dildo. But we also knew Dildo wasn't the ringleader. I need to see this through. For me. For the kids. James Sulpulveda. Damien Hafeman. Olive Tomms. And all the other kids we don't even know about."

"Right. That's why we're all here Em. All of us. But you can't put us at risk because of your wants and needs."

Her head dropped back against the headboard and she closed her eyes. She swallowed the emotion that clogged her throat and took a deep breath. "I swear to you, I will not put any of you in danger. I swear."

12

Chase finished his beer and started peeling the label on the next one.

Isaac leaned his elbows on the table. "Hey. Do you receive regular reports on the serum?"

"I do. Quarterly reports. Mostly they aren't anything new. We have a few test subjects and they are monitored, examined, and reported on. There has been nothing on the serum being sold off. And who would they sell it to? We were told it was to bring military personnel back to the battlefield faster. To reduce life-altering injuries and to eliminate the long-term effects of debilitating injuries."

"Such as?"

"Such as depression for one. Military personnel altered by lost limbs, internal injuries, lost hearing and sight would regain all of that. We had test subjects who we successfully attached severed limbs on and they, to date, are managing beautifully with them." He looked around to make sure no one was listening. "Emmy is a perfect candidate for this."

Isaac sat back and stared at him. He swallowed and took in a deep breath. "I'll check the system tomorrow. I have security clearance enough that I can see some anomalies or perhaps decisions made regarding the serum."

Shaking his head, he sat back in his chair. "I don't want you putting yourself at risk Isaac."

"I can always plead ignorance the first time. You know, 'oops, somehow I got into the system deeper than I meant to."

"It would be unbelievable for you to plead ignorance."

"We'll see. I'll also see if I can chat up the nurse I heard talking about it. She's in my department at the hospital. And she likes to gossip, so I think I can ferret out information."

Chase nodded and grinned at his friend. "Just don't get in trouble. I'm going to dig a bit with my contact too."

He took a swig of his beer then grinned at Isaac. "So, are you nervous?"

"About getting information?"

Chuckling Chase shook his head. "No dumbshit, about proposing."

Isaac laughed and his shoulders relaxed. "No." Then he began peeling the label from his beer bottle with his thumbnail. "Yeah. A little."

Both men laughed and the waitress made her way around to their table. "Another beer guys?"

Isaac shook his head. Chase then finished his beer. "I said I was buying dinner. Let's go next door to The Bourbon House and have some smoked ribs and slaw."

"Now that sounds like a dinner."

As they exited the bar Chase's shoulders relaxed at the same time a thought struck him.

"What's this nurse's name?"

They stepped outside and Isaac's brows bunched together. "What?"

"The gossipy nurse. What's her name?"

"Oh. Shelley Jasper. Why?"

"Hmm. Shelley Jasper. I think I remember her. She was at the hospital on base when I was there. I might see if I can run into her myself. Since we used to work together, she might be eager to share any news she has."

Isaac nodded. "Not a bad idea. Between the two of us, we should be able to gather a fair amount of information from her."

Chase opened the door to The Bourbon House and waited for Isaac to enter. "I'm not your fucking date Chase."

Chase chuckled. "Shut up."

The hostess smiled and greeted them immediately. "Two tonight?"

"Yes ma'am."

She led them to the back of the room, which was a relief to him, he was peopled out after the past three or more weeks. He sat with a thud and picked up one of the menus the hostess laid on the table.

"What about Emmy?" Isaac asked.

"What about her?"

"You still have feelings for her?"

He sat back with a thud. "I don't want to get all feely with you, but yeah, seeing her has jumbled up my insides."

"Did you tell her you came back to talk to her?"

"No."

"Why not?"

"She's still pretty pissy about the whole thing. She refused to stay or be admitted to the hospital, despite being in extreme pain. She wouldn't look at me that much and when she did it was with one of those 'if looks could kill' looks."

"She still has feelings for you."

"Yep. She feels like she'd like to kill me. And that was before the prescription."

"What does that mean?"

"I only gave her a two-day prescription for Vicodin. By now I'm sure she's found out and I'll bet she could cut through a grown man with the anger she's feeling about it on top of seeing me."

Isaac sat back in his chair. "Are you trying to get yourself murdered?"

Chase chuckled but shook his head. "I don't know what the fuck I'm trying to do. She had me all rattled and then refused to stay. And I wanted the opportunity to see her again when she wasn't so pissed off to try and help her. So, she'll need to come back to get another prescription."

"Geezus Chase, you're playing with fire."

A waiter stopped by their table. "Do you gentlemen know what you're having?"

Isaac ordered first. "I'll have a half-rack of smoked ribs with the slaw and add some okra to that order."

Chase wrinkled his nose, he'd never gotten used to the taste of okra. "I'll have the same without the okra. But I'll take a side of mac n' cheese."

"Sounds great. How about drinks?"

Chase grinned at Isaac. "We'll take a bourbon each. Make it the house bourbon."

"I'll be right back with those bourbons."

Isaac leaned back in his chair and stared at him a moment. "I think you should call and check on her. Soften her mood, it'll also help with her healing. Tell her you want her to come back in a couple of days when emotions and shock aren't so high and explain yourself. Then, chat about her treatment."

"What if she hangs up?"

"Call again."

Chase shook his head and chuckled. "God I shouldn't feel so new at this game, but dammit, she makes me feel like I've never dated anyone before."

13

Emmy sat in the front passenger seat of the SUV with her laptop open and on her lap. Her pain was managed, her mood hopeful, and she and her team had come to a solution for all of them. Kori sat behind her in the backseat to make sure she didn't leave the vehicle. At least that's what it felt like. The official reason Kori was here was to help her watch for movement and basically be her backup. Emmy was fine with the arrangement. She liked Kori and she did have drugs in her system. And it never hurt to have someone else helping out on this case. Hope opted to stay back at the house and make them all a dessert for their return celebration. It was also to keep her busy. She was still nervous about being out in public but as they all walked out the door, Emmy got the impression that staying in the house alone was a bit scary for her too. So, Kori came up with a plan. Now that they were parked and the guys had walked into the woods outside of the Smith home, Kori called Hope and she was on the phone listening so she didn't feel alone.

Emmy watched her laptop and the body cam footage from Diego, Falcon, and Creed. Her screen was parsed into four squares, with the fourth square showing her the overview of the compound in the daylight from overhead. Cyber had set this view up in their system so they could adequately make plans to capture Smith.

Kori whispered, "There's a vehicle approaching the compound."

Emmy looked up and saw the headlights beginning to brighten the road. It was only six thirty p.m. But it was dark now that fall had officially arrived.

"Sit perfectly still."

The vehicle continued moving toward them and she slightly held her breath. She pushed the button on her comm unit. "We have company. An SUV is coming down the road toward us."

Creed responded. "Roger."

She could hear her team breathing as they sped up and found places to stay hidden.

The SUV slowed as it neared the driveway and turned onto it without stopping.

Kori let out a breath. "Thank goodness we're tucked in the trees over here."

"Yeah."

Talking to her team she tapped her comm unit. "SUV turned up the drive and is now approaching the house."

Falcon answered, "See it. Emmy, when they stop the SUV I'll let you know, then start scrambling the cameras. I don't want to give them a heads-up just yet."

"Roger."

Emmy leaned forward and pulled the scrambler off the dashboard and put it on the console between her and the driver's seat. Twisting a knob and pushing a button, the unit turned on and activated itself to 'ready'. Emmy listened as she heard her team moving.

Diego spoke first. "There's an underground entrance behind the house. It looks like a garden shed, but the entire front opens up and the SUV just drove below ground."

Creed added, "I saw it from the side. The grade isn't all that steep and I'm headed out to the barn now to see if that's also a command center of sorts for Smith."

Falcon responded, "I'll come with you. Emmy, begin scrambling the cameras please."

Emmy pushed the green button and watched the lights blink. She could see one of their cameras high in the trees from her vantage point and she saw the light flash red on the top of it signaling it wasn't working.

She pointed it out to Kori who nodded. "Are you sure they didn't see us parked here in the woods?"

"I scrambled them as we drove up and until we parked. They likely thought it was a blip in their system. So, this will at first seem like the same thing and they'll likely believe they're having issues with their cameras."

"Except they saw you all here earlier."

"Yes. Except that."

Kori looked out the windshield and Emmy continued to stare at her computer and the body cam footage from her team. They now neared the door of the barn. Falcon's camera faced Creed and Diego and she saw them both nod. Creed took off and walked away from the other two and to the other end of the barn. Falcon turned in the opposite direction and began walking around the opposite side of the barn. Divide and conquer.

Creed's camera showed a service door on the other end of the barn and she saw his hand as he tried the door knob. It turned and he peeked inside. There weren't any lights on and Creed stepped inside. "I'm inside."

Emmy's heart raced as she watched her team step inside the lion's den. Kori inhaled and held her breath and Emmy nodded in recognition of that, but her eyes never left the screen.

Falcon whispered, "The door at the back is a large sliding door. It'll likely get too much attention."

Diego responded. "Don't open it. Someone just stepped out on the back porch and they're looking around at the cameras. Likely trying to figure out what's going on with them."

Creed whispered, "Come to the south end of the barn."

Emmy saw Falcon and Diego both move to that location and Creed stopped moving inside. "Camera above and to the right of the service door. Camera to the left and ten feet away from the service door. Three cameras at the north end of the barn. I'm going there."

Falcon entered the barn and Diego was right behind him. The three men split off in different directions, with Falcon walking up the middle of the barn, Creed to his right, and Diego to his left.

From the camera footage, Emmy and Kori could see boxes stacked in threes. Just high enough to reach the tops of the men's heads.

Emmy asked, "Falcon, what's in the boxes?"

He stopped and lifted the top of one of the boxes. "Papers." He scanned through them and opened another box. "Looks like tax documents."

Falcon then turned and the entire center lane in the barn was lined with boxes, all the same size, and all the stacks were the same height.

Creed warned, "Falcon, get out of the middle of the barn. That is lined as a roadway or path for a reason. We should know what that is before you walk along it."

Falcon turned and Kori let out her breath. Then the large barn door on the west side of the barn opened up and flashlights could be seen looking around the barn.

14

Chase listened as the phone on the other end rang. Once. Twice. Three times. Finally, he heard the ringing stop.

He tried again. Same result. Worry filled his body. He dialed her number again. Finally, a hushed voice responded.

"Emersyn Copeland."

"H...Hi Emmy. Emersyn. It's Chase."

"Chase, this isn't a good time."

"Look I know you're pissed but I need to explain..."

"Honestly this isn't a good time."

"Why isn't it?" He swallowed, she was going to make this difficult all the way.

"Look, we're on a mission right now and I have to stay alert. Call later."

The phone went dead and he sat for a moment staring at his television but not really registering what he was looking at. She was on a mission? In her condition? What the fuck was she trying to do to herself?

He stood and paced to his kitchen, then turned and paced back to the sofa. Unable to sit he turned again as he raked his hands through his hair and grabbed handfuls at the side and held on. He let a breath whoosh from his lungs before turning and walked toward his kitchen once more. He swallowed a large lump in his throat then stalked down the hall toward his bedroom. He quickly jerked his duffle bag from the corner of his closet and dropped it on his bed.

He gathered underwear, socks, and a couple of clean t-shirts from his drawers and dropped them into the corner of his duffle. From his closet he removed a pair of khakis from a hanger and a black three-button placket shirt and laid them on the bed. Folding them neatly, he placed them inside his duffle then stomped to his bathroom and pulled his toiletry bag from the shelf in his cabinet. Dropping that inside his duffle toward the opposite end of his clothing, he zipped his duffle and walked toward his kitchen. Pulling a few meal bars and electrolyte packets from his cabinet, he slid them into the side pouch on his duffle. He snagged a bottle of water from his refrigerator, picked his laptop off the coffee table and tucked it into his duffle, then turned off the television and the lights in his home as he made his way toward the garage door.

Once in his car he pulled up the address to the Airbnb Emersyn was staying at, and typed it into his maps app. Hospital records were a wealth of information. She was out of town, south of his location, but still in the State of Missouri.

He set his phone in the holder and waited for it to connect and direct him. His heart pounded in his chest right now. He had no clue what he'd say to her once he got there, but he hoped like hell Kori would help him out with Emmy and he'd be able to stay there to watch her until he could help her. That was incredibly hopeful on his part, but she wasn't taking it easy.

The GPS connected and he backed from his driveway and began his journey, which according to his GPS, would be an hour and fifteen minutes. That was barring traffic, animals in the road, and other hazards like broken-down vehicles, piles of rocks in the road, and other things that were common around this area; something he'd never really gotten used to.

Once he was on the road, he tapped the button on his steering wheel and when the robotic voice said, "Please say a command," he responded, "call Kori Jackson."

"Calling Kori Jackson on cell."

He grinned, because he'd have to change her name in his phone. But not today.

Her phone rang and she whispered. "Hi."

"Hi. Is this a bad time?"

"Yeah."

"Okay. Are you with Emmy?"

"Yeah."

"You're out on a mission? With Emmy?"

"Yeah."

"Okay." He took a deep breath and let it out slowly. "Look. I'm on my way to the Airbnb. She's got to take her condition seriously and it appears she isn't. I'm worried she'll do irreparable damage."

Kori didn't say anything and he got the feeling she couldn't right now.

"Can you call me as soon as you can talk?"

"Sure."

The line went dead and Chase shook his head. What the fuck kind of twilight zone had he stepped into today? Nothing about this situation was normal.

Shaking his head, he tried to focus on the road ahead of him and relax his shoulders. They were already bunched up and his neck was beginning to ache.

His phone rang and he tapped the answer button on his steering wheel without looking at his phone. "Kori?"

Isaac laughed. "Ah, no, now it's Kori? Man, you're beginning to give me whiplash."

"No, it's not like that. You know Kori. Kori Jackson, the woman I used to help with the trafficked victims she was saving."

"Oh, right. Sure. Sorry, are you waiting for her to call you?"

"I am, but if she does while we're on, I'll let you know."

Isaac chuckled and inhaled a deep breath. "So, I went back to the hospital after dinner. What you said was bugging the shit out of me and I wanted to get some sleep tonight. I looked into the computer and Project Superman has been canceled. I managed to get into it a bit, I could see some of the test subjects and the follow-up notes. I saw something that said "Kryptonite" and I clicked on that, but it was locked down. Then I clicked into an area that's labeled "Thor" and that's where the message pops up that says, 'Project Superman is now canceled'."

Chase's breathing sped up and his heart beat rapidly.

"When was it canceled?"

"It appears about three days ago."

Chase let out a long breath. "There wasn't a Kryptonite and a Thor."

"Ah, well, it appears they've taken your experimental serum and done something to alter it or change it and changed the project names. What do you make of that?"

He swallowed to moisten his throat. "I think Kryptonite might be how to stop the healing. I remember a vague discussion I'd overheard about that. I couldn't figure out why they would do anything like that."

"Right. Why would you stop anyone from healing?" Isaac cleared his throat. "What about Thor?"

"I'm afraid of what that might mean. My gut and my limited knowledge of Thor tells me he was stronger than Superman as a half-god half-human."

"Yes, that's my understanding as well."

Chase swallowed again and navigated a corner. "Isaac, thank you for checking on that. I'm going to see what I can do by way of research this evening once I get to the Airbnb."

"What Airbnb?"

"Emmy's."

"Whoa, you're invited to her Airbnb?"

"Not exactly."

Isaac chuckled and the line went dead.

15

Emmy's heart raced and she told herself it was due to watching her team, but she had to admit, Chase calling her had something to do with it too. As much as she didn't want that.

Diego, Falcon, and Creed crouched down as the men with flashlights entered the barn, then lights at the far end of the barn flickered to life. She saw the body cams as they scurried to hiding places among the boxes and she and Kori both watched as they held their breath. These were the times she wished she was there. It was less nerve-wracking than watching it unfold.

She ensured the scrambler was still working then had a thought. She flicked it on and off a couple of times and the lights on the cameras across from her clicked on to green then began blinking red again. The sound of someone's voice, not her team's, could be heard saying, "Yeah, here too."

For good measure, she flicked it a couple more times and the lights shut off and the door closed. Creed let out a deep breath, "I think they left. Nice job on the scrambler."

"Thanks."

Falcon began walking along the side rows of boxes and saw something shine near the floor. He pulled a flashlight out and shone it on the shiny object, then saw a wire. Emmy whispered, "Is it a trip wire?"

"Could be."

Diego moved closer to Falcon, his light flashing along the floor, "Here's another one. I'm following it."

Diego moved slowly along the wire, careful to see any others, should there be more. His light then followed a wire up the side of a wall, and to a box attached to the wall.

Falcon whispered, "If we shut off the electricity, will that shut off the power to the wire or do they have a generator?"

Creed whispered, "I'll look for a generator." The door opened and closed and Emmy watched Creed scramble around the barn on the outside. When he didn't find anything outside, he turned toward the house and Emmy's heart raced. It would be difficult to not be seen, they were watching outside now and soon they'd be on high alert.

Diego stopped and looked toward the front of the barn and a sliding noise could be heard. He crept closer to the sound, careful not to trip a wire and she could see a door in the floor raise and a man walked up a staircase from underground and onto the main level of the barn, the trapdoor then closed, and she could hear the soft motor running as it closed the door. She whispered to her team, "The generator might be below the barn."

The man turned on his flashlight then walked to a post along the middle aisle and flipped a switch, illuminating the barn.

Falcon and Diego dropped down and she couldn't see anything now but the sides of boxes.

Falcon rose just enough to see over a stack of boxes, though all they could see on the computer were the boxes.

He crouched down again and whispered. "He has a sensor in his hand. Emmy, if you flip the blue switch on the left side of the scrambler, it should scramble any infrared devices."

Emmy's fingers shook as she located the blue switch. She whispered, "Is this going to disrupt your cameras?"

"It's likely. But you should still be able to hear us."

She swallowed the lump in her throat and flipped the switch. "Done."

Kori leaned forward to see her computer screen better and they both watched as the cameras blipped on and off. "Can you hear me?"

"Yes. Shh."

A strange voice could be heard through the speakers, "Son of a bitch. What the fuck is going on here?"

Diego whispered, "He's trying to raise the trap door and it won't budge."

More swearing was heard then the door opened and slammed shut.

Falcon whispered. "He left in a huff in case you couldn't hear."

Creed chuckled. "He's stalking across the yard right now like a madman. Someone's in trouble. They should really buy better equipment."

The guys chuckled and Emmy couldn't help it, she did as well. It was funny.

Creed walked back to the entry door and slipped inside. "Em, if you turn the blue switch off when I tell you, I'll see if I can get that trapdoor to open."

"Creed, you need to be careful of those wires."

"I know. But I saw where he walked. It looks like the wires are only in one section."

"Okay, tell me when."

Her heartbeat sped up and she tried to moisten her throat but she felt completely drained of any moisture. Kori unzipped something in the backseat then reached forward and handed her a water bottle.

"Your throat is dry because of the Vicodin."

"Thanks."

Unscrewing the cap she took a long pull of water and felt the ice cold liquid slide down her throat. It was comforting.

Recapping the bottle, she set it in the cup holder to her left then watched the computer screen once again. After what felt like an hour, but was only a few minutes, Creed's voice was heard.

"Okay, Em. Turn the blue button off."

She inhaled deeply and let it out slowly then tapped the button off. "Done."

Their body cams came back on, and she saw the trapdoor lift. "I'm going down. Falcon and Diego, you two watch for them to come back out here."

"Roger."

She couldn't look away from Creed's camera and what they saw was both a puzzle and a wonder. Creed stopped at the bottom of the stairs and looked all around the basement, then pointed so she could see what he was looking at.

"Wow."

"There's our culprit. I'm shutting that generator down right now. Diego, can you prop the trapdoor open so I can get out?"

"On it."

"Em, as soon as I'm out, you need to hit the blue button again so if anyone comes out here with a sensor, it'll be scrambled."

"Okay. But I want to explore that basement much more."

"We'll come back tomorrow and we'll come back armed to the teeth. This is an unbelievable computer system down here and I'll bet it holds all sorts of records we're going to need to bring Smith down for good."

"Trapdoor's propped open."

Creed walked toward the generator and Emmy watched as he lifted a lid on the cabinet and twisted the off switch. He then reached in and pulled the spark plug from it. He then pulled a couple of wires and turned to make his way up the stairs.

Falcon said, "Creed, we've got company coming."

"I'm coming up."

Shots were fired and Kori screamed.

16

Chase pulled into the driveway at the Airbnb Emmy and her group were staying in. There were lights on and no cars visible. He swallowed because right now this seemed like a stupid thing to do. He was taking this far too personally, and he should just back away. Emmy was a grown woman, and she could do what she wanted.

Then a thought occurred to him. He tapped his phone and listened as the second ring ended. "Miss me?"

"Isaac, when you were in the computer, did you see the name of someone working on Thor or someone in charge?"

"Yeah. Dr. Calum Reid. I think I remember him from Fort Stewart."

"Yeah, he was there. Now he's at Leonard Wood?"

"Yep. They're working on it here."

"Okay. Thanks, Isaac. Enjoy the rest of your evening."

Isaac's low chuckle was all he heard before the phone disconnected. He sat staring out at the house and wondering what his next step should be. He'd like to run back to Fort Leonard Wood and talk to Calum Reid. But it was unlikely he'd be at the hospital now. Besides, he didn't want to get Isaac in trouble, and he'd need to log in and allow his sign in information to be attached to the project. He could easily say he was still interested in its progress. But he'd need to first contact, Dr. Karol Ember. She had already agreed to help him this afternoon. But she hadn't said a thing about Superman being discontinued.

He took a deep breath and put his SUV into reverse when an SUV pulled in behind him. Within a second of that, two big burly men stood on either side of his truck. Falcon Montgomery's very angry face stared at him from the driver's side and Diego, whom he saw at the hospital stood on the passenger side. His face was just as angry and unfriendly as Falcon's.

Swallowing, he rolled his window down and looked Falcon in the eye. "Dr. Chase Nicholas. Emersyn Copeland's physician. Kori's friend."

Falcon's jaw ticked then he stepped back from the door. "What are you doing here?"

"Emmy." He cleared his throat. "Emersyn isn't following my orders to rest. She's going to do irreparable damage. I'm worried about her."

"So you drove all the way out here for a house call? Or did you think you'd get in a booty call?"

"What?" His brows furrowed. "What the fuck is wrong with you? She's in no condition to..."

He shook his head. "I'm worried about her. I can help her if she doesn't deteriorate more than she has."

Falcon looked back at the SUV but stood stock still. Diego left his passenger window and he hoped he wasn't going for a weapon.

Falcon reached forward and opened his door. "Come on. Explain to Emmy why you're here. If she says you need to go, you'll need to go."

"Got it."

He stepped from his SUV and looked at Emmy, who stared at him from the passenger side of her vehicle.

He walked to her side of the vehicle and opened her door. Kori then stepped out of the vehicle and stood next to him.

"Chase. What are you doing here?"

"She's not taking care of herself."

"I'm doing just fine. I sat in the SUV and didn't leave it."

"How do you feel now?"

"I'm just..." Her eyes darted to Kori then back to him.

"Are you in pain?"

She softly cleared her throat. "A bit."

"On a scale of one to ten, Em?"

Her eyes locked on his and they held for a few moments. Hers were still as gorgeous as they had been years ago. Except he saw her pain. It was there. The rigidness of her jaw and the dark circles under her eyes told him all he needed to know.

"Eight."

"When was the last time you had a Vicodin?"

"Speaking of that..."

"Not now. We'll discuss that. When?"

He saw her eyes dart to Kori then back to him. She pulled a laptop case from the floor in front of her and grunted when she sat straight. Handing her case out to Kori, she then took in another breath.

"When Em?"

"About two hours ago."

"So, you had a Vicodin two hours ago and your pain is still at an eight?" he shook his head and his stomach plummeted deeper as the magnitude of her pain hit him. He swallowed the dry lump in his throat and softened his voice. "Em. I want to help you. I can help you. But you can't do more damage. You just can't for this to work."

A lone tear slid down her cheek, but she said nothing. He swiped her tear away with the back of his forefinger and whispered to her. "Let me help you."

He watched her throat convulse as she swallowed the fear and the tears she had welling up inside. They'd likely been there since the explosion, but she'd suppressed them deep down. Softer yet he said, "I can help you. I'll be here the entire time. We'll make it all right for you. I promise."

She sucked her lips between her teeth and after a long time her head turned and she faced him once again. "I know you're scared. I know you are so dedicated to your job, which is incredibly impressive. But I'm just as committed to my job and that is making sure you get better."

More tears spilled and she sniffed loudly as he watched her process. "You can be mad at me all you want. You can swear at me and hit me if you need to. I'll explain everything to you. But first and foremost, I want to help you." He laid his right hand over her folded hands. "Let me help you."

Her sullen, wet eyes looked into his and so softly it was nearly imperceptible, she nodded. Just once. But he saw it.

17

Emmy once again laid in her bed on her left side. This time, Chase had taken control of how to manage her pain.

"Kori, I need a pillow to place between her knees."

"Okay."

Kori opened the closet across the room and pulled two pillows from the upper shelf. She put them at the foot of the bed and waited dutifully for Chase to respond.

He looked into her eyes and a soft smile creased his cheeks. She saw his dimple. Gah! She loved his dimple. "Okay, we're going to continue to ice you down, which is why I wanted you to wear your sweater. We're going to keep it coming. Also..." He pulled a jar from his bag and set it on the table next to her bed. "This should help a little with the pain. It's topical and not likely to do much, other than offer opposing sensations to your brain from the heat it produces and the ice on your hip. It's aloe based."

"That sounds like mad science."

He chuckled and shrugged. "I suppose. But we've done some studies and it does help."

She held her hand out for the jar and he shook his head. "Either Kori or I will apply the cream."

"Why?"

"Because you need to do something else while this is applied."

"Really? Like what?"

He grinned and pointed to her phone laying in front of her. "Pull up your favorite music on your phone. I'll bet you have some Lynyrd Skynyrd on there. Or a whole host of songs from Darrel Worley or, perhaps, Zac Brown?"

She looked into his eyes for a long time, afraid to say anything because he had remembered the music she liked. Swallowing she picked up her phone instead and pulled up her music files. Scrolling to her "favorites" list, she tapped the link and the first song began playing. Darrel Worley sang about veterans and coming home and being at war and being changed forever and this song always resonated with her in so many ways. Especially after her accident. She was changed now forever. Physically and emotionally.

Chase chuckled and handed the jar to Kori. Kori pulled the blankets back gently, careful not to expose too much of her, and began applying the warming cream to her hip. While she did that, Chase lifted her right leg and tucked the pillow between her knees, stood back and looked at the angle of her leg then added the second pillow.

"Em, you can't stay on the Vicodin for long."

"I'm painfully aware you only gave me two days' worth."

"I wanted to make sure you would behave and take care of yourself. And..." He gently sat on the edge of the bed facing her. His eyes darted to Kori for a split second then back to her. "I wanted to have the chance to explain what happened."

Her stomach flipped and her breathing became stilted and taking a good breath became impossible. He leaned forward and put his hand over hers. "Just let me explain. Why are you avoiding it?"

She sniffed lightly, her nose tingled with the emotions running wild in her mind and her body. Her hip was heated and was actually quite warm now and it was nearly time for another Vicodin. But she felt the heat. The pain wasn't nearly as intense as it had been the past day and she was grateful for that. And tired. She finally felt like she might be able to sleep for a bit.

"Okay. Explain."

Kori put the lid on the jar and set it on the bedside table. "This is my cue to leave."

Emmy looked over her shoulder at Kori. "You don't have to."

Kori chuckled. "Ah, yeah. I do. I don't need to be in the middle of your shit here. Plus, I want to spend some time with my husband."

Emmy's shoulder fell limp. Kori and Falcon were still basically on a honeymoon and here they both were, not bitching and moaning, but working alongside her and taking care of her while they had a new married life to start.

"Of course. I'm so sorry. Go and spend time with Falcon. I'll see you in the morning."

Kori smiled at her then looked at Chase. "If you need assistance, you can call me."

Chase nodded and smiled and it was nice. He really did have the nicest smile. "Thanks, Kori. Enjoy your time with Falcon."

Kori stepped from the room and closed the door softly and Chase stared at the closed door for a long time. He stood then and picked up the ice bag from the foot of the bed where it lay on a towel and put a clean towel over her hip, then the ice bag. He pulled the covers up over her hip then and came back around to face her. Instead of sitting on the edge of the bed, he pulled up the wooden chair across the room and set it next to the edge of the bed so he could see her face clearly.

"I was engaged. She was back home, waiting for me to come back. We were high school sweethearts and I thought she was the one. We were young, gosh, eighteen when we got engaged. I was leaving for the service, and she was scared I'd find someone else. So, I proposed."

He clasped his hands together in front of him and looked at them for a long time. When he looked into her eyes again, he said, "Then I met you."

She scoffed and he held up his hands. "It's not a line. It's not a lie. You were...are different. You are self-assured. You came from a family that nurtured your confidence and abilities and you aren't afraid to jump into the gritty side of things. I was enamored by you the instant I met you. It sure didn't hurt that you're beautiful."

"Please. That's all so..."

"True. It's all true."

He took a deep breath. "I suppose I'd matured while in the service. I went home a few times a year, I called her weekly. Then it was bi-weekly. Then monthly. And she didn't complain. I went to medical school and she talked about moving out to be near me, but it didn't happen. I think we both matured. And I met you. We connected on mature levels. You loved talking about music and recon missions and life things. She talked about clothing and shoes and her favorite nail polish. You were the first mature woman I'd ever met that set off a spark in me. Man, Em..." He ran his hands through his sandy-colored hair, "you turned my head. We went to movies. We went bowling on base. We went to parties and you were...different."

He scraped his hands through his hair again and she felt a tear slide down her cheek and onto the comforter in front of her.

He leaned forward with his elbows on his knees. "We made love. It was incredible. So incredible. And, God, Em, I wanted you with every fiber of my being. All the time. But I knew it was wrong."

She sniffed. "You had an affair with me while you were engaged to someone else."

"Yes. And to prove you are the woman I thought you were, you didn't move forward with me. You asked me to leave."

She nodded but the water in her eyes made his form waver in front of her.

"But I came back. Two days later, I came back. I called Michelle and broke it off. The weird thing is she didn't even cry. We both grew up, I guess. I came back to your barracks to beg for your forgiveness and hoped you'd give me another chance, and you were gone. You took a volunteer deployment, and you were gone."

18

Chase sniffed and swiped at his eyes. Despite his best efforts, he still grew emotional.

"You didn't look for me."

He lifted his head and stared at her. Her gorgeous eyes looked tired, and her coloring was off. The pain was coming back. Probably pain in her heart as well as her injury.

"I kept track of you for a while. I knew you were in Afghanistan. I knew you were fighting hard. I decided to let you go because I didn't deserve you. I didn't know about your injury. Now, these past few hours I've kicked myself so many times for not following up. I could have helped you long before now."

"I wouldn't have let you. I was so damned mad at you. I still am. I was in love with you, and you belonged to someone else. You lied to me. To her."

She swept her hand through her hair and pulled it over her shoulder and behind her. Rearranging her pillow, she kept herself busy not looking at him, but he heard it. She was in love with him.

As soon as she'd settled once again, he looked into her eyes and smiled softly. "I don't deserve your forgiveness, but I sure do hope you'll offer it."

She swiped at her eyes once again with her right hand and took a deep breath. "I forgive you. It doesn't mean I'm not pissed at you still. It just means my parents taught me to forgive and not let the weight of anger hold me down."

"I can take that." He nodded. "For the record, I do understand your anger with me still. But I'll pray we are able to get past it."

Her full lips pressed into a straight line. "Your knees will be sore before that happens."

He grinned. "It'll be worth it." It was a start.

Glancing at his watch, he inhaled. "It's time for another Vicodin. Hopefully, you'll be able to get some sleep afterwards."

"I hope so too. I feel exhausted."

"Understandable. You've had quite the day."

He stood and walked into the bathroom connected to her bedroom. The Vicodin was on the counter. He twisted the cap and poured out one pill before closing the container again. Pulling the glass off the counter, he filled it with water and took them out to Emmy. She looked beautiful laying there. Her eyes sought his as he neared her, and he couldn't have looked away if he'd wanted. He sat gently on the edge of the bed and handed the pill to her. He felt the electricity when her fingers brushed his palm as she picked up her pill. Their fingers brushed when she took the glass of water from him and he tried not reading too much into it. But he hoped it was a way back to each other. A brief touch. A soft smile. Eye contact, all of those things meant so much when you were looking for acknowledgment from someone.

His phone buzzed a text message, and he pulled it from his pocket and read it. Isaac set up a 'chance encounter' with Shelley Jasper. Tomorrow at eight thirty am. Isaac was having breakfast with her and a couple of colleagues.

Chase grinned as he read the message from his friend. Emmy startled him when she broke the silence. "Good news?"

"Um, yes. I think."

"Yeah. Do you have to go?"

"Nope, I'll be right here all night."

"You mean as in here? This room?"

"Yep. It's an hour drive home and I need to be here with you to make sure you're okay."

"Chase..."

"Shut up Em. Just close your eyes and rest. I'll be here when you wake up."

He pulled his shoes off and set them alongside the bed. He went into her bathroom and brushed his teeth and used the toilet and when he'd finished and entered the bedroom once again, she was sleeping peacefully. He stood for a long time staring at her. The pain had left her face and she now looked like the Emersyn he'd known all those years ago. She was just like he remembered her in his mind. She'd changed very little from that time. Except, she had. She had an edge to her now she didn't have before. The innocence she'd looked at the world through back then was gone. She'd seen war, been damaged by war, endured so much pain, and seen so much sorrow over that time they were apart. But here she was doing good for people she didn't know and scraping scum off the streets because they did harm. Truly, she was a wonder and he was so fucking sorry for any of that pain he'd caused her. He'd caused them.

Inhaling a breath so deep his lungs burned he let it out slowly and softly lay on the bed next to her. Immediately her scent wafted over him. It was mixed with the minty cream on her hip, but he smelled her shampoo and her skin as it heated under the blankets. Her left hand was tucked under her cheek, but her right hand was between them and he gently reached over and laid his hand on hers. Her skin was still soft and he felt a thrill run through his body as their hands lay together. Just like they should have been all these years.

Tears sprang to his eyes again as he felt the gut punch of the remorse of his actions. He'd been wrong to enter into a relationship with her without breaking it off with Michelle first. He was stupid and his dread in making Michelle feel bad kept him from doing the right thing. But he'd never make that mistake again. Ever.

Now the stupid thing he was about to do was because it was right. Because she deserved to be helped just like she helped others. And, if he lost his medical license, so be it. Emmy needed him and he needed her, and he had the ability to help her. By God, he would do just that.

19

Emmy woke as the throbbing pain increased in her hip. She lay still listening to the sounds of someone breathing, her mind trying to clear itself of the drugs and sleep she'd been so deep into. Her mouth was dry and she moved her tongue around to find any bit of moisture.

Movement next to her froze her actions and a soft light on the opposite side of the bed turned on. Chase rolled over and looked into her eyes.

"Are you in pain?"

He glanced at his watch then to her again.

"Yes."

"Okay. I'll be right back. I'm going to get another ice pack from the freezer."

She let out a long breath and relaxed back into her pillow. More ice. She was tired of the ice. Her left side was beginning to ache from lying on it for so many hours. Chase crept toward the door and slipped out and she closed her eyes. Rubbing them gently with her right hand she hoped the itching would stop soon. For some reason Vicodin always made her eyes itch.

Chase entered the bedroom and approached the bed as silently as a mouse.

"I need to lay in a different position for a while Chase."

"Okay."

He gently lifted the covers over her hip and removed the warm ice pack and towel and put them at the foot of the bed. He moved the pillows supporting her back and laid them at the foot of the bed as well.

"Gently roll over Em. I'll support you if you need it, other-wise, try on your own."

She waved him away with her right hand. It was irritating being hovered over. “I've got this."

She tried not looking at him, but she caught the smile on his lips.

Inhaling a deep breath, she held it as she gently rolled to her back and let out the air from her lungs once she'd stopped moving. The multitude of sensations running through her body right now made her dizzy. Her left side tingled as circulation was restored. Sharp stabbing pains accosted her right hip and her back felt relief being able to stretch once again. She took slow steady breaths as all the sensations slowly drifted away. When she opened her eyes, Chase stood staring at her with the look of a doctor assessing his patient. That's when it occurred to her what bugged her about this whole situation.

He elicited feelings in her. The longing for what could have been. She'd missed spending time with him over the years. Dammit, she'd missed the hell out of him. Then, to protect her heart, she'd allow herself to get mad. Bone rattling mad at him for what he'd done to them. And a part of her, a large part of her, wanted him to have missed her. To have been so mad at himself for what he'd done that he couldn't forgive himself. But he'd finished med school and worked on premier projects for the Army and built up his career and that hurt her more. He'd moved on as if she didn't exist.

Now, he had inserted himself in her life once again and she couldn't shake the feeling that he saw an opportunity to experiment on her as if she were a lab rat.

Trouble is, she could benefit from the experiment, but it would likely rip her heart out in the end.

"Are you more comfortable now?"

"Yes."

He picked up the jar of cream on the nightstand and twisted the cap.

"I'll do it."

"No. I will."

"Chase, I can..."

"Shut up Em."

"Stop telling me that."

"Stop insisting you do the things I am capable of doing to help you."

"I don't like being hovered over or having someone do everything for me."

"I'm not doing everything. I'm doing what I can. At this moment, it isn't enough, but I'm expecting that at the end of the day tomorrow, or possibly the following day, I'll be able to procure the serum and we'll help you completely."

She swallowed as he warmed the cream between his hands. Then she watched as his hands touched her hip and rubbed in the minty cream. The combination of his hands massaging her hip and the warming of the cream on her skin gave her goosebumps. He carefully moved her panties up and smoothed his hand under the thin material to coat her entire hip.

Carefully, he replaced her panties and worked down her hip in the opposite direction and her breathing hitched. She felt like she couldn't inhale completely and it made her light-headed.

Chase wiped his hands on the towel he'd removed from her hip previously and sauntered to the bathroom for a new towel. When he came back to her, he put the towel over her hip, then laid the ice pack in the towel, then pulled her blankets over her, tucking them around the ice pack. The differing sensations once again made the pain lessen and she practiced steady breathing to help her relax.

"I can't give you another Vicodin for two hours Em. I'm sorry."

She looked into his eyes for a few beats of her heart, then shrugged her right shoulder but said nothing.

He picked up the glass of water on her nightstand and slid his left hand behind her head on the pillow and gently lifted until her lips touched the glass. She sipped at the water, enjoying the cooling liquid as it slid down her throat.

She tried drinking in more but he chuckled. "Not too much Em."

Her stomach felt heavy as his words once again denied her of something that was so important to life. Only this time it was water, last time it was him. She'd realized he was dishonest and that hurt more than anything else. Even though he explained why. It didn't change what had happened.

He laid her head on the pillow and set the glass on the table before making his way around the bed and gently lying on the opposite side of her.

"Don't you want to be under the covers?"

"I didn't want you to think I was being presumptuous."

She scoffed. "Cover up Chase. If you're going to take care of me, you'll need restful sleep and you can't get that if you aren't comfortable."

Their eyes locked a moment, then he stood, pulled the covers back, and slipped inside between the sheets, next to her. He turned the light off and turned on his side. She could tell he was facing her because she could hear his breathing. The moonlight streaming in through the top of the window turned his eyes silver in the light and she closed hers so she didn't see him anymore. Lying straight on her back, she practiced her breathing and prayed for sleep and help in keeping her heart from breaking once again. Somewhere between the two, she slept.

20

Voices in the next room woke him. He'd been up changing ice packs and attending to Emmy three times last night, the final time just an hour ago. She'd had a Vicodin then, and she now slept, though not peacefully. The look on her face showed him she felt the pain, though likely dull, it had been a presence in her life for a long time. She'd just learned to ignore it as much as possible.

He slowly rolled from the bed and stood. Turning to check that she hadn't woken, he then tiptoed from the room and out to hopefully get a cup of coffee and speak to Kori. He'd need her to help with Emmy while he met Isaac and Shelley Jasper. He also planned to connect with Dr. Karol Ember. She promised to help him get the serum. But he also wanted to know what she knew about Project Superman and the reason it closed.

As soon as he left the bedroom and the smell of the heating cream, the aroma of fresh coffee wafted to him, and he instinctively found his way to the pot. Cups had been pulled from the cupboard and lined up on the counter next to the coffee maker. He grinned and poured coffee into a cup, added a dash of creamer, and turned to see Kori, Falcon, and Diego outside sitting at the table chatting.

He opened the door and stepped outside.

"Good morning."

Kori smiled, "Good morning. How's Emmy?"

"Sleeping at the moment."

Diego nodded at him, then pulled the chair out next to him and nodded to it. His therapy dog, Ted, was next to him on the deck, and his tail wagged. Chase sat next to him and looked across the table to Falcon.

Falcon asked, "Did she sleep good?"

"She woke three times. I changed her ice pack and applied the Aloe to her hip. She managed well enough until she was ready for another Vicodin about an hour ago."

Diego took a sip of his coffee, then set the cup lightly on the table. "Can you really help her?"

"I can." He turned and looked Diego in the eyes. "I can."

"How? She's been told over and over again she isn't a candidate for surgery."

"She isn't. Her femur looks like a tattered flag. There's virtually not enough bone left to attach anything to it. But I led a team in the creation of a serum, it's injected, sometimes applied surgically, and it can be taken orally. It mends broken limbs, severed muscles, and tissues, including hearts and lungs."

"And why hasn't this been used on Emmy before now?" Falcon asked.

Chase took a deep breath and stared into his coffee cup for a long moment, then looked Falcon in the eyes. "I don't know. She was at Walter Reed where the primary test patients were located. She's a perfect candidate for it. I just can't figure out why she wasn't given the serum."

Falcon looked at Diego then back to him. "Who knows this?"

"I have a contact, who I'm meeting this morning who will hopefully shed some light on this very subject."

He turned to Kori. "Will you be able to help with Emmy while I'm gone? It'll be about three hours and when I come back, I hope to have the answers and the serum to help her."

"Of course. She's going to need more Vicodin as well."

He shook his head. "No. She can't have any more after today. Addiction is a real threat and if I'm able to obtain the serum today, she'll have to be off of it for twenty-four hours prior to administering the serum."

Kori's eyes rounded. "That's going to be agony."

"I'm afraid it will. But, once the serum begins to work, her pain will lessen. It'll be different pain, and there will be some, but it'll all be temporary."

Falcon heaved out a breath. "How do you know?"

"I'm the creator of the serum."

"No, how do you know the pain will lessen and that it'll be temporary?"

Chase nodded and lifted the bottom of his shirt up to expose his left side. "I was shot right here." He pointed to the slightly dimpled area over his rib cage. "It collapsed my lung. The bullet lodged in my ribcage and my colleagues and I were at a loss as to how to get at the bullet without collapsing my lung again and doing permanent damage. The serum was still in test stages at that time, and I insisted on being a guinea pig. Not only did my lung heal, so did my rib bone."

Falcon stared at his skin and Diego leaned forward to look at it as well. Falcon's eyes then met his, "Are they following your progress?"

"No."

"Why not?"

"No one but my colleague, Dr. Karol Ember, knows. She's the person who administered the serum and timed my progress."

Diego cleared his throat. "Why?"

Chase lowered his shirt and swallowed. "When I was shot, it was during a training mission and it was a wayward bullet. It's a bit of not wanting to get anyone in trouble and a bit of mad science that I wanted to be a test subject, but the serum was in its beginning stages and Karol and I hadn't gone to our higher-ups yet with what we'd discovered. So, we quietly administered the serum in the lab after everyone else had left for the day."

Falcon's eyes squinted and he bit the inside of his cheek. "So you were shot during a training mission, but no one else noticed? Then you quietly experimented with a serum you didn't even know would work?"

"Something like that."

Falcon sat back and crossed his arms over his chest. When his eyes bored into Chase's, his nerves went into overdrive.

"I call bullshit."

Chase let out a deep breath and closed his eyes for a moment.

"Look, I don't want anyone to get in trouble. Can we just leave it at that? The point is it worked. And we've since modified certain elements of it and used it on more than a hundred Marines and soldiers who have had miraculous recoveries."

Diego leaned his forearms on the table and played with his coffee cup. "So, why aren't you still working on this serum?"

"I was told by my up-line that they were happy with the serum and the project would simply continue as is. It was secret as they didn't want other governments knowing we had this technology in our tool belt. But they wouldn't be expanding on it, and I argued with them. When I continued to argue the benefits, I was reassigned. However, I receive quarterly reports on the test subjects and their progress."

Diego rotated his head, "So that brings us back to why Emmy wasn't a test subject."

21

Emmy finished her shower and Kori reapplied the Aloe cream. She dressed, then using her crutches, made her way to the living room where she could talk to her team and make a plan for the day.

She slowly sat in the recliner, then huffed out a breath. She was strong and practiced with crutches, but she hadn't slept the best and just that short walk exerted more energy than she realized it would.

Kori approached with a fresh ice pack in her hand and tucked it between the chair and her hip.

"Thanks, Kori."

She stood and smiled. "You're welcome. Let me know if you need anything. Hope and I are baking today. Do you like chocolate chip cookies or ginger cookies better?"

Laughing she said, "I love both."

"Okay. We'll make both. We're trying to stay busy."

Creed and Hope had made them all breakfast and Chase told her he had a meeting he couldn't miss then left early. Emmy inhaled deeply and let it out slowly.

She texted Creed, Falcon, and Diego. "Please join me in the living room, I'd like to discuss next steps."

Falcon, who had been sitting on the deck outside, immediately came in and sat on the sofa to her right, Diego joined them and sat next to Falcon and Creed sat in the armchair across from her.

She pulled up the reports from Cyber in their system and read through them. "Okay. Cyber hacked into Smith's camera storage. Did you all see the videos?"

They nodded and tapped on their laptops as they spoke. Diego was the first to verbally respond. "I think we go back and get inside that underground entrance. It's likely connected to the basement in the barn."

Falcon spoke, "By now they know we've been fucking with their cameras, and we shut off that compressor. They'll be watching closely. We only have one more shot at this before he skips town."

Emmy nodded, "I agree."

Creed tapped a few keys on his computer and they each received a ping. "I just sent each of you something I was thinking about last night. There's a little farm down the road from Smith's place, but according to the aerial map," their computers all pinged again, "there's a path of sorts that runs from one property to the other. They don't have cameras on that trail."

Diego squinted slightly as he looked at the GIS Map. "It looks somewhat grown up. Which means no one is using it. I think it's a good way for us to go in. We don't have to worry about anything until we arrive at this point right here." He clicked and added a pin from the map app and the others nodded.

She smiled. "We need Smith. Evidence gotten legally, so that will mean something on Smith that will tie him to the trafficking operation. That can be his phone with location responders at the shipping container company in Las Vegas, Miami, or anywhere else we know that's been used in the trafficking operation. Even those warehouses in Washington DC would be good. But, also tying him to the banks we know he's funneling money to."

Diego nodded. "I can bring that trail to the barn. Once inside, I'll follow the underground trail to the house. If someone sneaks into the back of the house via the secret entry, we can hit it up from different directions. Diego's therapy dog Ted's tail wagged. Diego leaned down and patted Ted on the head, "Yeah, you want to do that too don't you?"

Diego looked up at her. "Ted will go before me on the trail. Cyber is in their cameras, they can tell us via our comm units when they first see us. At that point, Cyber should have a fake video to play over their cameras of the empty field and no one on the road. It won't be real and will mask their true feed so we can get in. Plus, it won't alert them that someone is messing with their equipment. If something doesn't work, it's just a stray dog out in the field."

Emmy glanced down at Ted, whose tail wagged again then looked into Diego's eyes. "That's a fantastic idea."

Diego's cheeks reddened and Creed's grin stretched across his entire face. "That will work."

Once Diego and I are inside, Falcon, you'll watch the outside for any signs of someone approaching and stay close to the house in case you hear shooting."

"At that point, it's all-out war. We'll dispatch his people inside and lie in wait for Smith to come home if he isn't there now."

Emmy swallowed. She'd have to stay here. It killed her to do it. She so wanted to be part of this take-down, but she couldn't put them at risk. And Chase would be a pain in the ass if she tried to go. She needed to think about this more logically, if her team was worried about her, their attention would be divided, and if something happened, it would be her fault. "I'll have to stay here but I'll be on the computer watching the entire time."

Falcon closed his laptop and set it on the coffee table, then leaned his forearms on his knees.

"Em, that's honestly the best thing you can do."

She swallowed the lump in her throat and blinked rapidly as the moisture gathered in her eyes. Diego set his laptop on the coffee table. "Em, without you, we wouldn't have gotten this far. And this is a major trafficking ring we're stopping. You have been instrumental in all of it. All. Of. It."

A soft smile spread her lips. "Thank you, Diego. All of you, actually. Thank you to all of you. I'd always thought I'd be there to bring him in, but I couldn't be more proud of any of you."

Falcon stood. "Ditto. I'm going up to pack my equipment." He looked at Creed then Diego. "First dark?"

"First dark." Creed repeated.

Diego nodded and Ted wagged his tail.

Emmy read through the reports from Cyber and typed off the communication that would go to the entire team telling Cyber to prepare a still video from the footage they got last night and get ready to insert it when they saw Diego and Ted nearing the cabin.

She read the other reports from the entire mission, mostly to refresh herself on all they'd done in this case and to set her mind and heart at ease for not being there for the final takedown. But she'd been instrumental in the entire operation and it was time to let go, just a bit, and allow her amazing team the opportunity to shine brightly. She had no doubt they'd do just that.

22

Chase approached the table where Isaac sat with Shelley Jasper and another woman near the windows in the little cafe close to the hospital.

"Isaac?" He asked in his best-surprised voice.

"Hey, hey, Chase." Isaac stood and shook his hand then motioned to a chair next to him. "Please sit and join us."

As he sat, Isaac motioned to each of the women, "Shelley and Catherine, this is Dr. Chase Nicholas."

"Good morning." He greeted.

Shelley was the first to comment. "I worked with you, somewhat, at the hospital near Fort Leonard Wood."

He looked into her eyes and smiled what he hoped was his best smile. "You're right and I do remember you. Nice to see you again."

Shelley blushed and his spirits soared hoping she was flattered enough to want to impress him with all she knew.

"This is my friend, Catherine."

Catherine smiled and nodded. "Nice to meet you."

Isaac then took over the conversation. "Chase, we were just talking about some of the gossip at the hospital."

Chase chuckled, "I haven't heard hospital gossip from the base in a while now. Do continue."

Shelley scooted forward on her seat. "I was just going to say that Dr. Ember has been transferred and leaves tomorrow. She was working on a project that was just canceled. She's mad about it too. She snapped at the nurses yesterday, and that's not like her."

He responded. "I know Dr. Ember. She is the most composed person I know."

"That's what's so weird." Shelley added. "But apparently they're turning over all of her research to Dr. Calum Reid."

Chase nodded. Then Shelley gasped. "Wait, you worked with Dr. Ember on her experimentation of that serum. I remember when you left, Dr. Ember was really mad then too. Just like now."

Chase froze, Shelley did seem to know an abundance of information. Deciding to stop the conversation now, instead of digging in further with this gossiper, who would spill everything he said to anyone who would listen, he shrugged his shoulders. "That's the Army life I guess."

Isaac turned to Chase. "I asked Shelley and Catherine to breakfast this morning because I needed ideas for flowers for Louise. Shelley knows all about flowers of every kind."

Shelley rushed on. "Though he won't tell us what he's apologizing for, so it's difficult to select the perfect flower."

Chase chuckled. "He's been working long hours lately. Probably less of an apology and more of an 'I missed you' thing."

Isaac nodded. "He always knows."

Shelley excitedly began to rattle off flowers and the places to buy them and all sorts of nonsense he had no interest in. Right now, he wanted to touch base with Karol, and quickly, before she left base.

Chase patted Isaac on the back, "I hate to run, but I have an appointment and I just stopped in for a coffee to go."

Isaac laughed, "Yeah, no worries. Go on, and we'll talk again soon."

Chase stood and nodded to Shelley and Catherine. "It was nice seeing you, ladies."

He swiftly walked to the counter and ordered a coffee to go then pulled his phone out and texted Karol.

The clerk brought his coffee to the counter, and he paid her in cash leaving a nice tip, and hurried to the exit. Just as he slid into his SUV his phone chimed a text and he eagerly pulled it up to see it was from Karol.

I can meet now.

Where are you?

I'm just leaving the lab.

His heartbeat quickened. *Are you finished there?*

Not entirely.

He let out his breath in a whoosh. *Okay. Where do you want to meet?*

Come to my office at the hospital.

I can be there in fifteen minutes.

He took a couple of deep breaths and began driving from the parking lot. As he drove, he ran through his mind what he'd need if he had to recreate the serum on his own. There were ingredients he had at his disposal, then there were a couple of them that could only be found at one or two big pharmaceutical companies in the US. He tried running through his mind who he knew at either of those companies that he could contact should Karol be a dead end now.

Deciding to stay positive he silently prayed this would work out. It would take him weeks to procure all he needed to recreate the serum and he'd rather not wait. Emmy's hip wouldn't make it much longer before she'd be in a wheelchair.

He pulled into the hospital parking lot and parked toward the back, needing to get some steps in. He could use the fresh air and the exercise to work off some of his nervous energy.

He strode to the doors and slipped easily into an open elevator door. Pushing the second-floor button he stared straight ahead and prayed once more that Karol could help him.

The doors whooshed open, and he stepped into the corridor to the second left. Her door was ajar, but he knocked anyway, and she quickly pulled the door open and ushered him in. She then closed and locked the door behind him.

His brows furrowed as he watched her. When she turned to face him, her brown eyes were filled with worry, the dark circles ringing them, a tell she hadn't slept well.

"Hi."

She tried to smile, but it didn't work, so instead, she held her hand out to a chair in front of her desk, then she took her seat behind her desk.

"Hi. Sorry for all the cloak and dagger."

Shaking his head he looked into her eyes again. "I heard you've been transferred."

She scoffed and shook her head. "They want me away from here. From anything to do with Superman."

"Why?"

She leaned in and her voice lowered. "Someone up the chain of command has sold it off to a crooked pharmaceutical company."

"Why?"

"Money." She rubbed her forefinger and thumb together indicating the same.

"What about the Marines and soldiers it's meant to help?"

She ran her hands down her face, trying to wipe away the worry. Huffing out a breath she said, "They were only guinea pigs. Lab experiments. A means to an end."

"I don't understand. Our parameters were clear. We were helping Marines and soldiers get back on the battlefield faster. We were ending depression by healing these men and women. We were doing good for those who do good for us."

"That's absolutely what we were told. And what we were doing. But someone got greedy."

"I don't understand who they'll sell it to."

"Athletes. Someone wants super athletes."

He sat back in his chair as if he'd been punched. "What the fuck."

"That's what I've been saying since yesterday when I was dismissed from the project and told to pack and leave."

"Where are you going?"

"I think Hinesville, Georgia."

He stared straight ahead at the wall behind her where a photo of her family used to hang.

She opened the top drawer of her desk, then pulled a key out and opened the top drawer on her right.

She pulled out a small black zipper bag and set it on top of her desk.

"This is the third generation of the project. And, just so you know, the reason I was asked to leave is because I questioned it. I questioned the sale and had a bit of a fit over not helping our military. Just as you did. I should have learned, but I can't stomach this."

He nodded. "Yeah. I was just thinking of what I'd need to recreate it on my own."

Her eyes sparkled for the first time. "I was too. I have the contacts."

He leaned forward. "We can do this Karol. We'll help our men and women out, without these assholes."

"That's why I wanted to meet with you." She pushed the black bag toward him. "I have what you'll need to help Emmy. And I have two more doses for you to keep for us to use as samples. I'm sorry to ask you to guard this, but they'll be watching me. I was lucky to get this out yesterday when my lab partner went to the bathroom."

"I'll guard it. With my life, if I have to."

"Once I'm settled, I'll contact you. We'll chat then. I'm also not re-enlisting. So, in eight months when my contract is over, I'll be out. We'll work on it then."

He tucked the black bag into his inside jacket pocket and stood. "I look forward to hearing from you when you get settled. And, thank you so much. Emmy really needs this."

"I'm happy to help her."

He started toward the door then stopped. "Do you know why they wouldn't have used it on her at Walter Reed?"

She pursed her lips and stared at him. "Text me her full name. I'll look in the computer when I get to Hinesville."

"Thanks, Karol." He hugged her small body and felt her shaking. "I'm so sorry this is happening to you. You're a top-notch doctor."

"So are you. They don't care. It's about the money. But we'll win in the end."

23

Emmy had moved around the living room today. Starting from the recliner. Then the sofa. Then to the armchair. And back to the recliner. Every time she needed to use the bathroom or needed to move because she was sore, she moved to a different spot.

She now lay in her bed, just waking from a Vicodin-induced nap. She rubbed her eyes and ran her tongue around her mouth trying to revive any moisture that may still be present. Unfortunately, Vicodin depleted her body of moisture.

Slowly pulling the pillow from behind her she gently moved to her back and waited for the pain to settle before trying to sit up. She glanced at her watch and saw that she had another two hours before she could take another Vicodin and then she'd be down to two more. Then what would she do?

Heaving out a breath she pushed herself up with her arms and turned to hang her legs over the side of the bed.

Giving herself a minute to orient herself she reached for the glass of water on her nightstand and took a long drink of water.

Waiting for her body to take all it needed, she set her near-empty glass on the table and reached for the crutches leaning against the wall near the head of the bed. Taking a crutch in each hand, she used them for support while her left leg handled the bulk of the work.

After positioning a crutch under each arm, she steadied herself then made her way toward the door.

As she neared the door, the aroma of freshly baked cookies filtered into the room and, her stomach growled. Twisting the doorknob, she pulled the door open and inhaled the full aroma of the baking going on in the open-concept kitchen/living room, and it was heavenly.

Chase sat at the breakfast counter eating cookies and both Kori and Hope chatted away while they either added more cookie dough to the baking pans or took freshly baked cookies off of one.

Kori looked up first and smiled. "Come on in and have some fresh goodies."

Chase turned and smiled at her, and her heart raced. Probably the drugs.

"Hi, you look rested. Did you have a good nap?"

She focused on her path toward the counter and not falling before saying anything. Once near a stool, she slid onto it gingerly and let out a breath. "I did have a good nap." She didn't look over at him. She couldn't right now.

Wouldn't. She didn't want to look at his handsome stupid face.

Kori set a clean glass in front of her and poured some milk into it. "Just a small amount so your stomach doesn't get upset."

Hope plopped two cookies onto a plate, one of each kind, and put them in front of her. "So far, everyone has a favorite and has been eagerly eating them before we can even put them into a container. I'm glad you woke up before they are all gone."

She chuckled. "Those guys do know how to eat."

Falcon came down the stairs, "I heard that. Sheldon doesn't bake cookies with real sugar in them. Don't get me wrong, he's an amazing cook, but, Emmy, real sugar!"

He nabbed another chocolate chip cookie from the cooling sheet and Kori lovingly slapped at his hands. "You'll ruin your dinner."

Chase chuckled then asked. "Who's Sheldon?"

She finally turned to look into his eyes and her tummy rolled over and butterflies swarmed inside. "He's our chef."

"You have a chef?"

"Otherwise who would cook? We're on the road and eat at different times. He keeps us fed and he makes delicious..." She glanced at Falcon. "Healthy meals. We have to stay in shape, and he does his part."

She bit into the first cookie and closed her eyes and enjoyed the flavor of the warm chocolate chip cookie. She let out an "mmm" and Falcon laughed.

"See. Sugar!"

"Yes. It's delicious. You ladies did a beautiful job."

Chase chuckled. "So, Sheldon keeps you all healthy food-wise. Does this mean you all live together or do you all meet up and eat at a designated place?"

"I built a compound. It's not what it sounds like though. It's actually a large building that houses all of us, or those of us who want to live there. We have ten apartments, a huge kitchen, a common living room, and dining room. We have our offices underground for security. Right now, not all of us live there. Donovan and Hadleigh live at her house. Charly and Sam live at his house. Diego and Shelby and the kids live there though. Deacon and Becca live there but are looking at buying a house of their own. Mia and Caiden still live there but are also looking to buy a house. Piper and Royce have their own home. Falcon and Kori are still there although they haven't been there more than a couple of days since we've been on the road. And..." She looked at Hope and smiled. "Hope and Creed haven't had a minute to think about anything like where to live. They're planning a wedding and I think Charly is helping Hope's parents look for a house in town too."

Hope nodded. "That's true. They found one yesterday they really like and are putting an offer in on it today. I'm waiting to hear from them to see if their offer is accepted."

"That's exciting."

Hope smiled. "It is. It'll help to settle in with my parents so close."

Chase sat back and looked around at the group of them. "Wow, I'm impressed. That's fantastic."

Emmy shrugged. "You know for us," she pointed to Falcon and herself, "and the other operatives, it's what we're used to. Living on base or in a barracks while deployed is what we're used to. So, when we created RAPTOR, it was easy to see us living in close proximity. Plus, my Uncle Gaige's company, GHOST, is right next door and many of them live there as well."

"That's very impressive. I can see how it makes it easy for work."

Diego came downstairs and set his bag near the front door. "I'm set to go. We should leave in about an hour."

Falcon looked at his watch and Emmy did as well. Falcon nodded, "I'm all packed. I'll go get my things."

Kori and Hope began cleaning up the cookies. Hope said, "I'll get supper going. You all need to eat before you go."

24

Impressive. That's what she was. Emersyn Copeland was an impressive woman. She'd built a company from the ground up and she was stopping traffickers. It was people like her and the operatives who worked for her, he and Karol had thought they were helping. They, and all the Marines and soldiers they worked with all these years.

When he'd questioned some of the decisions surrounding the Superman project, he'd been unceremoniously dumped. Actually, in Army terms, he was transferred to another base and he'd decided to not re-up when his contract was up a few months later. He focused on helping civilians who needed it and those military personnel and former personnel who found him. He still received the reports, and he wondered if those were even real. He had no claim to the scientific data that had been collected, he was an employee of the US Army. Even the countless hours he'd put into the work wasn't his. But he'd make sure from this point on, it would be. When Karol finished up her contract, they'd recreate a new batch of the serum, and they'd help everyone who needed it.

"Chase?"

He blinked and saw Emmy staring at him with her eyebrows pinched together. His head jerked back slightly and he took a deep breath.

"Sorry. I was thinking of something. I didn't hear what you said."

She pulled herself up to her full sitting height and swallowed. "I only have two Vicodin left. What happens next?"

"Okay. Let's have a chat about that. Do you need to move to a more comfortable chair?"

"Yes. That would be wonderful."

She pulled her crutches to her from their resting position against the counter to her right. Using them to steady herself, he watched her face as she stood. His eyes dropped down to her legs and feet and he saw she was only resting on her left foot.

When moving to the recliner a few steps away, she didn't use her right leg at all, but bent her leg at the knee, and pulled her foot up behind her.

He strode to the freezer and pulled a fresh ice pack from inside, then brought it in to her. As she reclined the chair back, she pulled a towel from the arm of the chair, and he wrapped the ice pack in it, then set it between her hip and the chair. He then sat on the coffee table in front of her.

"I have the serum. You'll need to be off Vicodin for twenty-four hours before I can administer it. Usually, and especially in a case as severe as yours, I'd prefer to do it at my clinic where I have a nurse available to help me. I'll make a small incision in your hip, directly over the worst portion of your femur, and apply the serum directly to the bone. I'll also inject a small amount of the serum into your system for it to travel through your body and find all the areas that are damaged. It'll heal them. In two days, I'll re-Xray and see what's happening. There will be some pain as the bone regrows and mends itself. The muscles and tissue that are damaged will tingle, maybe itch as they're mending themselves. Each patient is different."

"Are you shitting me? You have something like that and you aren't using it on everyone?"

"Right. Those are my thoughts also. Karol's too. But it's actually property of the Army."

"Who is Karol?"

He hid the grin at her question because it came out with a tinge of jealousy attached and he liked that she might be a bit jealous of another woman where he was concerned. "My lab partner and the doctor with whom I developed the serum."

"Where is she?"

"She's being transferred to a new base as we speak."

"To work on the serum?"

He scraped his hands through his hair as Falcon, Diego, and Creed came into the room to listen. "No. She's been fired, so to speak. The same as me."

Emmy's eyes rounded and her brows shot up in the air. "You were fired? You mean discharged? From the Army?"

"No, I wasn't fired or discharged. At least not until I chose to leave at the end of my contract. I questioned some of the decisions around the serum and I was immediately transferred to another base. And by immediately, I mean that very evening. They didn't want me poisoning Karol or any of the other lab staff. But, when she's off duty and I am as well, there's no way they can stop us from talking. I called her and told her what happened and now the same thing is happening to her."

Falcon ran his hands down his face and Diego shook his head in disgust.

Creed stretched his shoulders. "Glad I'm a SEAL. That's some dirty shit going on there."

Chase turned and looked at him. "That's not the worst of it. They've canceled the project we called Superman. Rumor has it they've sold it off to a pharmaceutical company. It was developed for Marines and soldiers, not athletes."

Diego scoffed. "If there's money to be made, someone will find a way to make it. It disgusts me that someone who is supposed to be helping us sets us aside for money though. But it isn't the first time at all."

Emmy looked into his eyes. "How did you get the serum then?"

He bit his lip and hesitated, but in his heart, he knew this group would never say anything. "Karol snuck it from the lab for me." He held his hands out to her. "For you actually."

He felt guilty about not telling them about the extra serum, but he wasn't ready for that information yet.

"She could get court marshaled for that." Emmy said quietly.

"Only if she's found out. Right now, she's in the clear. We have a signal if either of us gets in trouble and she hasn't signaled me, so I have to believe, she's safely on her way to Georgia."

"Okay. So, I have two Vicodin left. I'm not taking either of them. By this time tomorrow night, we should be able to do the procedure and we'll have Smith in custody, so I'm all in."

Falcon looked up at Kori who stood in the kitchen listening and she nodded.

Turning to Emmy, Falcon said, "We'll get him tonight. It's our last chance and we'll stay at the cabin until he comes back. No matter how long it takes."

25

She stared into Chase's eyes. The lines between his brows warned her of concern.

"What's wrong?"

"Nothing." He shook his head once and started again. "Only, I want you to really think about this. If it doesn't work or if something goes wrong, you won't have any repercussions."

"What could go wrong? Be straight with me."

"In the test subjects, which appears to be everyone we've used the serum on, it didn't always work. Some of them didn't see any improvement. We were trying to keep track of them and study their lifestyle, diets, and medical history. There must be some correlation and commonality in them. It's worked beautifully on the majority. I just want you to be prepared."

"So, worst case scenario, it won't help me and I'll be in a wheelchair and have to figure out how to do my job differently. Best case scenario, it'll work completely. Mid-case scenario, it'll help a little bit and I'll have some improvement." She shook her head, "I don't see the downside, other than a bit of disappointment."

She looked at her teammates and one by one they shrugged or nodded.

"Diego. Do you feel good about the plan tonight?"

"Yes. I think it's solid. And Cyber just uploaded a report on the banks they've tied him to. All we need to do is get him. That will be a pleasure."

She nodded and glanced at Creed. "How about you?"

"I'm ready and believe we'll get him. Once we dispatch his employees, we'll hold them hostage until they tell us where he is and when he's coming back."

"What if they're loyal and won't say a word?" She grinned.

Creed chuckled. "It might be very painful for them to not say a word."

Falcon and Diego chuckled, and Chase squirmed.

"Okay, Falcon. How confident are you about tonight?"

"I'm all in. We have a solid plan and as soon as we have Smith, we'll have his cell phone. The first thing I'll do is plug it into Cyber so they can run all the data on it. We'll find his waypoints, his banks, his passwords, his whereabouts. I know it's going to work."

She inhaled a deep breath and made eye contact with each of her teammates, then with Chase. She lingered on his eyes the longest. Her heartbeat sped up and she tried, unsuccessfully, to ignore the thrill of having him close again. She would be a fool to trust her heart to him.

"I'm as confident as these guys are."

He nodded, his eyes staring into hers the entire time. "Okay. I'll call the clinic and have Quinn set up the surgery for tomorrow evening."

"I take it Quinn is your nurse?"

"Yes, and a damned good one. Discrete, which is essential, especially in this case."

She nodded, then Hope announced supper was ready and Falcon clapped his hands together. "Okay, let's eat up and go get a fucking piece of shit for dessert."

Creed laughed and Diego grinned but shook his head. She glanced at Chase to see his reaction and he laughed along with Creed.

Chase stood and waited for her. "Do you need assistance standing?"

"No."

"You don't have to be tough all the time Emmy. It's alright to need help and it's alright to ask for it."

"You're kidding me, right? Everyone has been helping me since we got here. Before here even."

"There's a difference in you needing the assistance because you can't do it on your own and the assistance being offered would be a great help even if you can do it on your own. In other words, I know you can do it on your own, but wouldn't assistance be kind of nice?"

Creed nodded, "He's got you there, Em."

"Shut up and go eat," she snapped, but Creed just laughed then wrapped his arms around Hope and kissed her forehead.

Swallowing, she looked up at Chase, who stood waiting for her to ask. Smug bastard. Dammit, why did he have to be right?

"Yes, I would appreciate the help."

He stood beside her, a beautiful, sexy, warm smile on his perfect lips, and held the crutches out to her. "Here take these. I'll help support you under your arm and once you are standing, I will steady you while you get the crutches under your arms." She nodded, scooted to the edge of the recliner, put her feet on the floor, and mostly using her left leg, stood.

They were so close when she stood. She could smell his aftershave, which smelled just as fresh as if he'd just applied it. His eyes this close were still the beautiful hazel she'd so long ago looked into and had fallen in love with. And they stared directly into her eyes right now.

Her heart felt a stab and her hands tingled just from his touch. She swallowed a lump in her throat and saw his Adam's apple bob as he did as well. Her left leg began to shake slightly, and she shook her head to get her emotions under control.

"I need to sit down."

"Not yet. Hang on. It is just a few steps to the kitchen. I've got you."

He let go of her right hand as he reached down and picked up her crutches from their resting place against the side table. Holding them up before her, she took a deep breath and placed the crutches, one by one, under her arms and leaned on them.

Her body began to sweat and she told herself it was from the exertion and not Chase, but those two things were beginning to blur in her mind.

Hovering behind her, he gave her the space to head to the counter where she planned on eating. Falcon, Kori, Creed, and Hope sat at the small table in the corner, Diego at the end of the counter, and Ted ate from his bowl nearby. That left two stools at the counter for her and Chase.

She picked the stool at the end of the counter because it was easier to sit on. Taking her time, she managed to sit fairly comfortably and Chase walked around the other side of the counter and pulled bowls of potatoes and creamed corn, and a plate of roast beef toward her to fill her plate. She refused to look at him as she filled her plate, which wasn't all that full, but her appetite was suppressed today. Likely from the drugs.

Once she'd finished, Chase filled his plate, then looked at Diego, who shook his head and kept on eating.

Chase walked around the counter and sat next to her and dug into his food. Light conversation floated around her but all she could think of was Chase. He was sitting next to her and eating a meal as if they'd been together all this time and her heart constricted once more.

26

Chase sat on the loveseat to Emmy's left, glancing at his phone. He'd sent a text to Karol to see if she was alright and had made her journey without issue. He now waited for her response.

Hope and Kori sat on opposite ends of the sofa, both on their phones and Emmy sat in the recliner on her computer waiting for the guys to let her know they were in place.

None of them seemed totally at ease. They were all simply passing the time until the action began, and it was eerily nerve-wracking because he was not used to this at all. Kori and Hope seemed as uncomfortable as he was. Kori's feet were on the coffee table, but they moved back and forth at a quick pace. Hope bit the cuticles on her fingers and alternately played with a lock of her hair. Emmy was the only one who seemed totally comfortable with the situation.

Finally, Emmy looked up at the television screen and tapped her computer. "They're in place."

Her computer screen was displayed on the television as she turned up the volume. She muted her computer so the guys couldn't hear them, then she reminded all of them of the rules.

"Don't forget, if I unmute, they can hear us. No worrying comments or statements, just be quiet so we don't take their focus off of the mission. It's for their safety."

Hope and Kori nodded then she turned to him. He nodded, "Understood."

Diego's voice was first to be heard. "Ted and I are in place."

Falcon responded. "I'm in place. Near the back entrance."

Creed then announced, "I'm in the barn and just slipped down the trapdoor. No one is down here."

Emmy held up her hand to show them she was unmuting then tapped her computer. "I have a visual on each of you."

The television screen split itself into four squares showing the body cams on each of the operatives and one visual was a camera showing the driveway.

Ted showed on Diego's camera and he ran along the path between the farm behind the Smith house and the house. Ted's dark coloring made it tough to see him sometimes, but he stopped often and turned around to make sure Diego was still following him.

Chase moved to sit on the edge of his cushion and watched each of the cameras one by one. Creed's camera showed the basement area under the barn and it was filled with computers and it looked like the operations for the security systems. There were boards lit up with green and red lights, some of them blinking. He found a doorway and began slowly walking down a tunnel. His camera was infrared, and everything looked an eerie greenish color.

Falcon's camera showed him slowly turning back and forth to look all around him. His camera also turned to infrared. Other than it being dark, it seemed peaceful and calm.

Suddenly a light above Falcon clicked on and Emmy began tapping on her computer. She held up her finger briefly and unmuted her computer. "Camera's spotted Ted. Cyber is placing the fake footage onto Smith's cameras now."

Diego's voice lowered and he whistled quietly to Ted who turned and ran back to him out of camera range.

They each gave a thumbs-up in front of their cameras and halted. Emmy's computer pinged and she unmuted her microphone and said, "All clear. Fake footage is up. Proceed."

Each of them began their previous activities. Diego and Ted made it to Falcon's location. Falcon nodded at Diego then motioned with his thumb to the doorway. Falcon proceeded to the doorway and Diego and Ted stayed outside, watching for anyone approaching.

Falcon's camera showed him trying the doorknob only to find it locked. He then pulled a small tool, presumably from a pocket, and inserted it into the lock. Just a couple of twists and it unlocked. He turned to Diego, who nodded and gave him a thumbs-up.

As quiet as can be Falcon slipped inside of the house. Chase couldn't stop watching Falcon's camera. Kori moved and he saw her out of his peripheral vision standing up and moving toward the television. She wrapped her arms around her waist.

Falcon moved down a hallway toward a room with a light on. He turned to look into a room on his way on the right, which was a small kitchen. Dirty dishes were stacked on the counter, but it wasn't a total mess. He continued on down the hall toward the light and a floorboard creaked. He froze and waited and a voice from the room called out, "I'm almost finished with the funds transfer."

Emmy typed feverishly into her computer and he suspected she had Cyber on the bank transfer. Falcon stopped just outside the doorway of the room and waited. A chair squeaked and he stepped inside, his gun held in front of him and a shot was fired.

Kori squealed and he glanced to make sure she was alright and then looked back at the television. The body camera was obstructed by hands and material and more material. It was clear a fight was playing out before them and he hoped the man on the computer wasn't nearly as strong as Falcon.

Finally, a loud thud and then another and Falcon stepped back and his body cam showed a man lying on the floor, blood on his balding head, his face looking away from the camera. Falcon heaved out, "I shot him in the leg, he's now unconscious." He turned his body cam to the computer.

"Bank First Southern, it looks like forty-five million dollars is being transferred. Should I stop it?"

Emmy unmuted her microphone. "No, Cyber is patched into your body cams. Just stay in that position until they can capture the numbers."

He glanced at Kori whose shaking fingers tucked a lock of hair behind her ear. Her eyes never left the screen.

Diego said, "Someone's approaching. I'm coming in Falcon."

Diego's camera showed the back of the house and then the door opening. Ted entered first and Diego followed him down the hall and toward Falcon. He turned the corner to move into the room with the computers and Falcon gave him a thumbs-up.

Falcon then said, "A car door outside just closed. I'm going to need to move soon."

Emmy unmuted. "Go ahead, Cyber has what they need."

Falcon leaned down and picked up the injured man's feet and dragged him to the side of the room against a wall by the door. Diego stood against the wall by the door and Falcon stood across the room facing the door. Ted lay down next to Diego.

Footsteps could be heard entering the house.

27

Emmy's heart pounded in her chest and her hands sweat as she watched her team complete this mission. She didn't feel as bad as she thought she would not being there, but real fear surged through her body at watching from afar. She adjusted herself in the chair and a sharp pain shot down her leg and up her hip. She grunted but managed to keep it low and made a mental note that as the Vicodin wore off she'd feel the pain more and more.

Chase left the living room and walked into the kitchen. She heard the freezer door pull open and in a few seconds, he was reaching in alongside her and the chair and pulling the old ice pack out and replacing it with a new one. She paid attention but also watched the screen and the footsteps grew louder.

A man stepped into the room and froze when he saw Falcon. Diego faced Falcon and the look on Falcon's face was murderous. Diego quickly hit the man upside the head and he dropped like a hot rock. Falcon ran over and pulled the man into the room. They looked at his hands and arms and found a watch and pulled it off his arm. Diego checked for weapons and found one at his side and one in an ankle holster.

Diego pulled zip ties from his pocket and tied the man's feet together and bound his hands behind his back. Together they pulled him into the room further. Both were breathing heavily from exertion. Creed reached a doorway and it opened to a set of stairs.

"I found the steps to the house. I'm coming up."

Diego replied, "Roger."

The man Falcon had shot began to move and Falcon pulled out zip ties and bound his feet and hands together. The man moaned but Falcon didn't stop.

Diego looked at the watch he'd taken off the second man and scrolled on it.

"This man here is Travis Preston. He's Smith's bodyguard. Or one of them."

Falcon found a phone on the man near the computer and opened it up. He held the phone to the man's face, and it unlocked the phone. Falcon shrugged and scrolled through the phone. "This here is Tito Hogan. Cyber do you have any information on him?"

She watched them typing into their messaging system then unmuted her microphone. "He's on Smith's payroll as an IT person."

Falcon nodded.

Creed walked down the hallway and entered the room. He looked at the bodies on the floor then grinned. Diego nodded and the three men had a moment. A brief moment.

Diego looked at the watch in his hand. "A message from Smith. Says he's on his way back. Make sure Tito sends the routing information forward to his phone."

Falcon glanced at Tito's phone as it buzzed. "Send the routing info."

Falcon spoke to Emmy. "Em, Cyber needs to send him the routing info and make it look like it's from Tito."

"Okay. Forward the message to Piper."

Falcon forwarded the message. Emmy watched her computer, waiting for confirmation from Piper. As soon as she got it, she unmuted again. "Delete Piper's number from his phone, she got the message. In a minute you'll see the message pop up on that phone as if he just sent it."

"Roger."

It didn't take long. Her Cyber team was simply the best. Caiden then sent a message across the chat. "Message sent."

Falcon nodded and turned the phone to his camera so she could see it at the same time she received Caiden's message.

She held her breath for a few seconds. Her pain level was increasing and so was her anxiety. They just had to get Smith.

Falcon looked at the phone again then at Diego and Creed. "He's on his way."

Falcon then directed the team. "Diego, you and Ted should go into the bedroom across the hall and hide. Creed, you go into another room and hide. I'll do the same. Once he comes into this room, we'll all rush in. I don't want him to see anyone until he gets to this room.

Diego and Ted went across the hall and Creed and Falcon both found other rooms to hide in. The house was incredibly small, and it didn't take long to hide. Falcon was in the kitchen and Creed in another bedroom. Lights hit the windows as the car pulled into the driveway. Falcon looked out the window in the kitchen and said, "He's driving a Cadillac CTS. Looks like he's alone."

He then ducked behind a doorway and the back door opened. Footsteps could be heard on the comm units and two steps went into the kitchen, then backed out and went down the hall. The footsteps echoed down the hallway in the quiet house. He likely thought it was too quiet and someone on the run would be wary of every place all the time. He stopped before entering the room where his employees lay then he turned and stepped inside. He quickly turned to run out, but all three men were on him in short order, and Ted barked up a storm then clenched his teeth into Smith's pant leg.

Smith could be heard swearing and struggling. He didn't go down easy, he fought like his life depended on it and it actually did.

Emmy's heart raced as she watched, she jerked and moved without thought, and pain sliced through her body, but she didn't care. Her breathing came in spurts and she grew incredibly warm and sweaty. Finally, they'd wrestled Smith to the ground and Diego bound his legs and hands behind his back and Falcon and Creed then slid him into the room with his employees.

Falcon turned so his camera was on Smith. "Got him Em. We got the motherfucker."

Tears flowed down her cheeks and Kori and Hope cheered and hugged each other. Emmy swiped tears from her face but they were quickly replaced with more. She tried taking a couple of deep breaths, but her lungs were constricted and she wasn't able to.

She closed her eyes a moment and let some of the adrenaline settle then swallowed the lump in her throat and unmuted her microphone. "Thank you so much. All of you. Terrific job. Just terrific."

With shaking fingers she picked up her phone and tapped out a message to Casper and her Uncle Gaige who were waiting to hear from her. "We got him."

28

He knelt alongside the recliner that Emmy sat in and he took her hand in his. Looking directly into her eyes he smiled. "Congratulations Em. God dang it, congratulations."

She smiled at him. Genuinely smiled. It took him back to those days so long ago when she smiled at him all the time. Her eyes were wet with tears, her lashes spiked and her nose was reddened. But she'd never looked more beautiful than she did at this moment.

Her breathing still came in spurts and he said, "Hey. Follow my breathing." He inhaled slowly and then let it out slowly. He still held her hand tightly and he nodded when she followed along and did as he asked. "Again." Inhale slowly then exhale slowly.

He nodded again and she smiled. She let out a breath and nodded at him. "Thank you."

Her phone pinged and she looked at it.

She pulled her hand away but this time it was slowly not like he repulsed her.

Looking at the message on her phone she smiled softly at him. "I have to work."

"I know. You do what you do. We'll just watch."

She slightly giggled then unmuted her microphone. "Casper is sending someone from the base over to take care of the interrogation. Cyber has the banking information. Does he have a phone on him?"

He watched the television again to see her operatives, which seemed appropriate right now after he just witnessed what they do, begin to search through Smith's clothing. Diego pulled it from a pants pocket. "Here."

"Okay. Plug it into your phone and open the RAPTOR portal. Cyber will pull all the information from it they need."

Smith began swearing that he'd have them all in jail and Falcon kicked him in the stomach, only hard enough to make him shut up. "There'll be more and in more uncomfortable places if you don't shut the fuck up."

Smith opened his mouth and Falcon's foot reared back. Smith clamped his lips shut and Falcon nodded. Thank goodness Creed stood facing Falcon so they could witness all of this. It was incredible. All his time in the service, he never had to complete a mission quite like this one and those smaller ones he did complete were so long ago he worried he wouldn't be able to remember how to do it anymore.

Emmy's phone rang and she answered, "Hi, Uncle Gaige."

Her tears began spilling again and he grabbed the box of tissues on the side table and set them alongside her on the small table next to her. She smiled, at least that's what it looked like, but she was trying hard to hold back the tears as her uncle undoubtedly congratulated her on a job well done. She nodded a few times but said nothing, and he wished he could hear what her uncle said to her. She sobbed a couple of times and swallowed and he remembered that this was the first time he'd ever seen her cry. She was always so tough and stoic. This really hit her hard.

"Okay." She managed to say into the phone. "Thank you."

She tapped the end call button on her phone and sniffed. Pulled a tissue from the box and blew her nose, then unmuted her microphone.

"Casper's person is named, Lia Landon and she'll be there in about twenty minutes. She's getting the full-blown emergency treatment and is being helicoptered in. Sit on Smith."

Diego said, "Roger."

Ted lay at his feet, and Diego leaned against the wall with his gun still in his hand. Tito began moving around and moaned a bit. Falcon turned him over and saw that his leg was bleeding. He took his backpack off and pulled a medical kit from inside and tied a tourniquet around Tito's leg above the wound, though it didn't appear to be bleeding that bad.

"Probably going to need an ambulance here, Em."

"I'll call them."

Kori said, "I can do it, Em. You keep these guys doing what they need to do to come home."

Emmy smiled at her and nodded. "Thank you, Kori."

He smiled at Kori as well and she walked over and hugged him briefly, then stepped into the kitchen and called for an ambulance.

Chase looked down at Emmy who watched him closely, then he smiled. "That was hard on her and Hope."

Emmy glanced at Hope who still stood near the sofa watching the television and Creed on any camera she could see him on. Emmy nodded at him then and took a deep breath.

He sat on the coffee table, near Emmy, a straight view to the television. As they say, "it ain't over till it's over" and this wasn't over until Casper, whoever he was, had Smith in custody.

They had a little lull as they simply watched the television screen, the text conversations in Emmy's chat session were flying past quickly, her team congratulating each other.

"Who's Casper, Em?"

She looked at him and cocked her head slightly to the side. "He's our contact at the State Department. He's worked with my Uncle Gaige for years and is who actually hired GHOST to help the military when jobs were outside the lines the military can cross. It's what helped GHOST grow so quickly and prosperous and I think he also had something to do with the Agency hiring RAPTOR. Some of this," she pointed to the television, "is out of his realm, but he puts us in contact where we need to be and he plows the way through all the red tape for us when needed. He's been a dear, valuable friend to both organizations."

Chase nodded. When she spoke of Casper her expression changed. She genuinely admired and respected him. She really did have some great contacts.

Sirens could be heard through the microphones and Emmy unmuted again. "The ambulance cannot come in until Lia arrives. They'll need to wait outside."

Diego responded. "I'll go out and explain it. Ted can take a break then as well."

Diego and Ted left the room, and they watched him walk down the hallway to the ambulance just pulling into the driveway.

29

Emmy watched Diego speak with the EMTs. Clearly, they were upset but understood there was still an active situation going on inside. Meanwhile, her pain level was rising, and she needed to move to a different position.

She set her computer on the table next to her and Chase jumped up to help her. "What do you need?"

"To move. I have to recline more for a while."

"Okay." He stood before her and handed her the crutches, then moved to her left side. Holding the crutch grips in her right hand, she inhaled deeply, then stood. She cried out as the movement sent sharp pains running up and down her leg and hip.

"I've got you."

His strength was welcome. His body heat seeped into her body and his strong arm circled her and made her feel secure and supported. She stood still and waited for the pain to subside, then she took a deep breath and pulled away from him.

"Okay. I'm okay now."

She put one crutch under each arm and began the slow trek to the sofa. Kori came in and brought some pillows from her bed to prop her up, "Thanks, Kori."

"Of course."

She carefully sat on the sofa, then turned and reclined against the pillows. She took some deep breaths as the pain subsided. She let out a long breath as she settled and watched Chase bring her laptop to her.

In that short time, Diego and Ted had gone back inside and Falcon, Creed, and Diego stood silent as sentinels at the doorway of the room where Smith and his employees lay on the floor.

Travis Preston had now wakened and was looking around and squirming in his bonds. He glanced at Smith and started to say something, but Creed stepped between them. "No!"

Falcon then spun Travis around so he faced the far wall and couldn't see Smith or Tito.

Smith then glanced at Tito. Clearly, he expected his employees to help him. Creed then took the chair that Tito had been sitting in previously and placed it between them so Smith couldn't see Tito. Emmy's phone rang and she answered it on the first ring.

"Emersyn Copeland."

"Ms. Copeland, my name is Lia Landon and I am an intelligence officer sent to speak with Anton Smith by Casper. I will be pulling in the driveway of the Smith home in three minutes."

"Thank you, Ms. Landon. There is an ambulance in the driveway as well. One of Smith's employees was shot in the leg, but we told the ambulance he couldn't be moved until you arrived and secured him."

"Thank you for the update. I have officers with me who will escort Mr. Smith's employee to the hospital and secure his room. Please tell your team to expect me now."

"Will do."

Emmy hung up and unmuted her microphone. "Lia Landon is pulling in the driveway now. She has intelligence officers with her who will secure Tito and escort him to the hospital and secure him."

Her operatives each gave the thumbs-up and Smith began to swear another blue streak, which earned him another kick, this time a bit closer to his nether regions and it shut him up immediately.

They saw the lights swing past the windows in the house and Kori let out a long-held breath. Hope sat on the edge of the loveseat but continued to stare at the television screen without blinking. At least it looked like she wasn't blinking.

A door opened and footsteps approaching the operatives could be heard. It sounded like she came with an army. In reality, it was actually only four others.

Lia Landon asked Diego and Creed to lift Anton Smith up to a sitting position on the sofa so she could speak with him. He fought them every step of the way which earned him a hard slap across the face and a harsh jerk from Diego. He and Creed then lifted him under the arms and roughly plopped him on the sofa. He leaned forward and refused to look at Lia Landon. Creed shoved him back and warned him. "I'm serious as a heart attack Smith. Sit your ass up."

Smith slowly rose up but shot a deadly look at Creed, who responded with a chuckle.

Hope spoke for the first time all evening. "He's so bad. I've never seen him behave like this."

Kori responded. "They have adrenaline running through them by the gallons right now. They have no way to expel it, so they're doing what they can. Plus, they each want to kill Smith in the most horrific way, so I think they're behaving very well."

Hope grinned at Kori. "I meant bad in a good way."

Kori laughed and hugged Hope. "I get it. They are bad."

Chase glanced at Kori and grinned and her cheeks flushed.

Chase's lips spread across his face in the most handsome smile she'd ever seen, and she'd seen so many breath-taking smiles from that man. "It looks good on you Kori."

"What does? Lust?"

"Love. Lust. Whatever it is, you look truly happy. It looks good on you. I'm incredibly happy for you."

"Thanks."

He turned and looked at her, and she felt sucker punched. Her breathing shallowed and she had a hard time taking in air. Her body heated and she felt her cheeks flush and heat.

Then something crashed on the television, and they all stared once again as Travis Preston kicked at the table where the computer was set up and it crashed to the floor. Diego leaned and grabbed his feet while Falcon cleared the way and Diego slid him across the floor until he was laying in the middle of the room. Finally, two of the intelligence officers leaned down and picked Travis up under his arms, and stood him on his feet. A third officer joined them and they took him under his arms, the third picked up his feet and the taller of the officers said, "We'll secure him in the vehicle."

Lia nodded and Diego looked at Creed and Falcon. "Ted and I will supervise."

Emmy's phone rang and she picked it up and saw Deacon's name on her screen. "Hey, Deac."

"We have everything from Smith's phone. We have it all. He was at the container yard in Vegas. He was there when Piper was taken. That day. He was on the boats when Hope was there. We have him. And, we have his banking information. We have payouts to the Congressman. Em, we have it."

30

Chase watched Emmy's face change from smiling to her lips quivering as she tried holding back tears. She bit her bottom lip and swallowed then took a deep breath and said, "Deac. Say it again. I'm putting you on speaker."

Tapping her phone she turned and looked into his eyes. "We have all the evidence from Smith's phone that we need to convict him. We have it all."

A tear trailed down her cheek and their eyes locked. She swallowed continuously and he saw her hands shake as she held her phone.

Her voice cracked when she responded. "Send it to Casper please."

"Will do. Congratulations, Em."

She shook her head. "Congratulations, Deacon. Tremendous work by all of you. Every single one of you."

He chuckled and cheering could be heard in the background. Shuffling sounds were heard then a female voice came on the phone.

"Em. It's Charly. Congrat-u-friggen-lations! We did it Em. We got him."

Emmy sniffed and he turned and grabbed the tissue box once again and set it next to her on the sofa. When their eyes locked, his heart swelled in his chest. She was admirable. She was impressive.

She pulled a tissue from the box and dabbed her eyes then swiped her nose.

"How are you feeling, Charly?"

"I feel fine in the evenings. The mornings are tough though."

"It'll pass."

Charly laughed. "That's what I keep telling myself. How's Kori?"

Emmy looked up at Kori who stood near the kitchen counter watching the television.

"I'm good Charly. Only a little queasiness in the mornings. Not bad though."

Emmy smiled at Kori then her eyes dropped to his and her smile grew just a bit more.

"Okay, I'm jumping off here. The guys are still in the field. Take care of yourselves. We'll have a party when we get home. We have a lot to celebrate."

"When are you coming home?" Charly asked.

She looked at him and he shrugged. Then whispered, "Three or four days."

She repeated the timing then said, "I'm having surgery tomorrow. Surgery of sorts anyway."

"Oh Em. What can we do?"

"Start planning a homecoming party so we can celebrate a hard-fought mission accomplished, babies, and weddings. Plan it all. Work with the others so every celebration is included. We've had to let so much go without a celebration for the past two years."

Charly laughed. "We'll plan it. But if you need something, please let us know."

She stared into his eyes. "Chase and Kori will keep you all informed."

He smiled and nodded at her and a single tear slid down her cheek. "Gotta go Charly."

"Bye, everyone."

Just before Charly hung up the cheers in the background rose up.

Emmy pulled another tissue and watched as Lia interrogated Smith. For his part, Smith refused to say anything at this point despite Lia's continued questions.

After some time, Lia turned to Creed and said, "We'll take him in. We've brought armored vehicles and we'll transport them to base where they'll be held until charges are filed. Casper will be down here in the morning, and he'll make the final call."

"Em, did you hear that?"

"I did. Thank you, Ms. Landon."

She smiled briefly. "You're welcome. Well done."

The pride in his body swelled beyond anything he'd ever felt before. These people! Amazing was the only word he could think of now and that was so inadequate. Then she tried adjusting herself on the sofa and he saw the stab of pain hit her. Her brows scrunched together, and her jaw clenched.

He walked to the kitchen to change out the ice pack. The least he could do was keep her iced and as soon as she knew her team's involvement was completed at the house, he'd get her to let him put more heating cream on her hip. He didn't want to be creepy about it, but he took pleasure in applying the cream to her hip. Her skin was soft and he enjoyed touching her. Helping her was now his new mission. If he had a mission, that's what it was.

He went into the bedroom and pulled the covers back to ready the bed for Emmy. He washed his hands in the bathroom they were sharing, though it couldn't have been more platonic if they tried. That made him sad. He had no one to blame but himself. He'd lied to her and let her go because he didn't feel worthy of her. He'd changed the trajectory of both of their lives, and he'd paid for it every day since the day she told him to take a hike. He'd followed her career for a while afterwards, but then it became too painful so he stopped.

His phone chimed and he pulled it from his pocket to see a text from Karol.

All clear. I'm in Georgia now, Dan and the kids will follow me in a few weeks when he gets the house on the market.

Thank you for letting me know. I've been worried about you.

No need. All good. How is Emersyn?

He took a deep breath and sat on the wooden bench in the bathroom. *In pain. Using the heating aloe and ice packs. Serum tomorrow.*

I know you know this, but you can use a pain blocker for a few hours tonight to help her rest. She'll need to be rested and healthy tomorrow.

Yes. I have it. I haven't told her about it because I don't want her asking for it early.

We've had enough experience to know that is a smart move.

Thank you, Karol. Take care of yourself.

I will. I'll be around tomorrow if you need anything. I don't report in until Tuesday.

He sent a thumbs-up and pocketed his phone.

He stepped into the bedroom and pulled his bag from the closet floor where he'd stashed it. His black medical kit was hidden in a secret zippered pouch within, and he pulled that out now. He then texted his nurse, Quinn, to affirm all was ready.

She responded within a minute. *All set. No patients will be around, the clinic will be closed to all. Privacy ensured.*

His stomach twisted like never before. He wanted this for Emmy. He wanted to help everyone, but this one was incredibly special. She was everything.

31

Her team was on their way back and according to Hope and Kori, they were within a few minutes of arriving. She pulled her crutches toward her and gritted her teeth as she moved to set her feet on the floor. She would stand for them when they came home. She would honor all they'd done for this cause, this company, and all the victims who'd endured years of horror.

Kori rushed over. "Em, let me help you."

"I can do it. Just stand close in case I fall."

Kori shook her head. "You don't need to be so tough, we're a team."

"I do. For all my team has done for me over the years, I do."

"They do it because they believe just like you. You gave wounded warriors a purpose and a mission in life, and they all live it and feel it."

Hope came into the living room and smiled. "She's right."

"What you two don't understand is in the beginning, there wasn't a lot of money. They worked for next to nothing until the agency brought us on. They sacrificed their bodies and their lifestyles to build RAPTOR."

Kori laughed. "Listen to you. You think they are the only ones who sacrificed? You did as well and with a lot more on the line. You signed huge loan papers because you believed in them. Falcon told me he'll never regret a day working for RAPTOR."

Hope looked at Kori and nodded. "Creed said the same."

A lump the size of Mount Everest formed in her throat, and she couldn't wait to get back to her normal non-emotional self. She was tired and worn, and in so fucking much pain it made her teeth hurt. And she wanted a shower.

Using her crutches as her brace, she used her left leg to help her stand and she did it without crying out. She did huff out a breath once she positioned the crutches under her arms.

"After I welcome the guys back, I need a shower. I can't go into surgery without taking one."

Kori laughed. "I was thinking of that. There are plastic lawn chairs in the garage. I thought we could put one in the shower and you can sit and shower yourself. "I'll help you in and out."

Hope nodded. "I can help too. I want to help."

The door burst open and three smiling faces entered the house. Falcon was first and he rushed to Kori and spun her around. He kissed her lips and they laughed together. Creed entered behind Falcon and sought out Hope, scooping her in his arms and kissing her lips.

Diego and Ted came in last. Ted rushed to her and she bent the best she could and scratched him behind the ears. She smiled at Diego and held her hands out to him. He hugged her tightly and she whispered, "Thank you so much for all you do."

He pulled back and his eyes were wet. He nodded, "Same to you."

Falcon came over and hugged her then Creed.

"I want to hear all about it. We saw it, but I want to hear all about it. But it'll need to wait until tomorrow morning. I thought we'd do a video conference with the entire team. GHOST wants to participate too according to Uncle Gaige."

Creed grinned. "That would be wonderful. My nerves are shot right now, but in the morning we'll all feel ready to explain it all."

She huffed out a breath and started moving toward the bedroom door. "I need a shower and a nap."

Kori and Hope both stepped away from their husbands. Kori hurried to the garage door and Hope followed her to the bedroom. Just as she approached the door Chase opened it and stepped out. They bumped into each other and his arms immediately wrapped around her shoulders to right her.

"I'm sorry."

"It's alright. I'm going in to take a shower."

"Emmy it's not..."

Kori entered the room with her white plastic chair. "I've got it, Chase. She can sit in the shower. It's important for her to feel clean, she'll rest better."

Chase nodded then stepped back. "As soon as you're finished, I'll apply the heating aloe and an ice pack. I do have a pain blocker I can use to allow you some rest for the night. Only one and it'll last approximately four hours."

She relaxed slightly on her crutches. "You don't know how good that makes me feel."

He grinned and she thumped past him with Hope and Kori behind her.

Kori passed her by, "Let me get this set up in the shower."

Hope then asked, "Em, where are your clothes?"

"I have them in my bag on the chair."

Hope walked to her bag and pulled out clothing for her. She didn't care what she picked, she just felt gross now. She'd been sweating and then cold from those ice packs, then sweating again. Her emotions had been on a roller coaster for the past couple of days and her pain made her lose reason sometimes. Last night when she woke, she noticed Chase had rolled to her and she almost kissed his lips. She'd missed his kisses so much over the years. Oh, he was a fantastic kisser. She heard the door close and turned her head to see he'd left the room. Her heart deflated. It felt like their breakup all over again so many years ago. Her eyes teared up but she took a deep breath and blinked rapidly to dry her eyes.

She continued into the bathroom and decided to cry in the shower and cleanse herself of all the bad memories, all the emotions, all the everything so she could go to sleep and wake feeling ready for whatever was next.

Kori motioned for her to sit on the wooden bench, then immediately began pulling her shoes and socks off. Emmy pulled her shirt over her head then reached back and unfastened her bra. She'd been in enough barracks over the years where modesty wasn't a thing, there wasn't time to be modest.

Kori stood and grabbed a big fluffy towel from the closet and wrapped it around her shoulders.

"I need you to make your way over to the shower now and before you sit, unbutton and unzip your pants. I'll get them pulled down and you can sit. I'll get the water warmed then hand you the shower head. You can take your time from there. Hope and I will be in the bedroom waiting for you to finish."

Taking a deep breath, Emmy stood and gritted her teeth against the pain. She immediately began to sweat, and her towel fell off her shoulders. Kori picked it up and re-wrapped her. The shower was luckily a zero entry, which relieved her immensely. Her plastic throne sat inside waiting for her and she grinned. She limped along to the chair, then turned slowly and set her crutches against the wall. Kori quickly undid her pants for her, then tugged them down her legs. Her panties were next and as soon as she had them down, she nodded to her and Emmy slowly sat in the plastic chair.

Kori pulled the shower wand from its cradle and pointed it at the wall until the water had warmed. Once she had the water temperature regulated, Kori handed her the shower wand and nodded. "Take your time, Em. You deserve it."

The two women left her alone in the shower and she leaned her head back and let the warm water wash over her long hair. She then sprayed her body and let the tears fall.

32

Chase prepared the syringe with the serum and placed it on the table with his instruments. Usually, Quinn would do this, but she was prepping Emmy right now. They'd slept very little last night, Emmy was uncomfortable, even with the pain blocker. She couldn't go another day like this.

Lining up his instruments, he mentally used each one with success, closed his eyes, and sent up a prayer for steady hands, and a successful surgery. Of all of them he'd performed in his years as a physician, this one meant more to him than any other. He wanted a successful outcome for all of his patients, but especially Emmy. He owed her this. And, if he were being honest, he wanted to be the one to help her. He wanted to be the one she thought of every time she stood, or walked, or moved without pain. If she wouldn't give him a second chance, he at least wanted her to know it was him who helped her. But, he wanted a second chance. He needed a second chance.

"Dr. Nicholas?"

He turned to Quinn. "Yes. Is she ready?"

"Yes, she is."

He took a deep breath and nodded. "Okay, bring her in and prepare for surgery."

Quinn nodded and disappeared, and he covered his tools with a sterile cloth. He changed his gloves. The door opened and Quinn pushed the bed into the operating room, Emmy was lying on her back, her eyes seeking his.

"I see you haven't changed your mind." He joked.

Shaking her head, "No. I need this. I want it too, but I need it."

He nodded. Quinn locked the gurney in place and walked around next to him. Together he and Quinn grabbed the sheet under Emmy. "Okay Em, we're going to pull this sheet and slide you onto the operating table. Lie still, don't try to help us or move in any way. We've got you."

Her voice shook slightly. "Okay."

Quinn counted, "One. Two. Three."

They pulled together and slid Emmy onto the table. She groaned as she jostled slightly but said nothing.

Her hair was tucked under a hospital cap, and her legs stuck out from under her hospital gown. Her eyes had dark circles under them from lack of sleep and pain. But he'd be a happy man if he could look into her dark brown eyes forever.

He laid the back of his hand against her arm. "I'm going to give you a light anesthesia to help you relax and rest. Everything I do from this point forward will be for your comfort. It should only take us a half hour and we'll get you into the patient room you just came from until you wake. We'll both be by your side the entire time. Okay?"

"Yeah." Her lips parted into a smile and her eyes looked into his for a long time. He didn't look away, he wouldn't until she did. Then she smiled again and said, "I trust you."

The lump in his throat nearly cut off all his air. She trusted him? After what he'd done to her, she trusted him.

He blinked rapidly because his eyes grew wet, and he cleared his throat before speaking. "Thank you. You'll never know what that means to me."

She nodded and closed her eyes, and he took that as a sign to get things rolling.

"Quinn, let's begin."

Quinn handed him the syringe with the general anesthesia, he opened an alcohol pad, cleaned the tube on her IV, and inserted the needle. He watched the heart monitor as he squeezed the entire syringe into the line that put Emmy into a nice sleep state. He watched her face as her breathing evened out and enjoyed it as her face softened from her pain-pinched brows and her jaw relaxed.

Quinn added the blood pressure clip on Emmy's forefinger, pulled her gown back only far enough to expose Emmy's hip, and rubbed the area with the iodine tincture to sanitize it. He felt relaxed as he picked up the scalpel and made the opening to expose her damaged femur and hip socket.

Once exposed, Quinn handed him the first syringe of serum and he found with his fingers, each split in the fractured bone and applied the serum directly. Once he'd finished with the femur, he moved to her hip socket and applied the serum, ensuring the entire area was covered. He closed her up, then applied serum to the stitching and the final dose of serum would be injected into her hip to find any places he'd missed.

The serum, once injected into a body had proven to be powerful in most of their test subjects. They'd watched it the first few times under X-ray and found that the serum became almost alive on its own. It blended with the body's red and white blood cells and used them as a vehicle to travel through the body. Anywhere it found a weak spot, the serum filled in and healed. He and Karol had been amazed and also a bit terrified of what they'd created. But, years later there'd been no horrible side effects. Just the opposite, their test subjects had done splendidly. Of the few who did not, the worst of it was the serum did nothing and they'd never been able to research why. The Army told them that wasn't the purpose of the project. His irritation and argument to that were what had gotten him removed from the project. But Karol kept him updated as much as she could and the reports he still received filled in some gaps.

Quinn applied the gauze bandage over Emmy's incision and cleaned up the iodine while he watched Emmy's vital signs to ensure she wasn't experiencing any reactions from the serum. His breathing was steady, much more than he thought it would be. His fear that this wouldn't work for her had been what kept him up the last couple of nights.

After thirty minutes, he felt safe in moving her to the patient room. They transferred her to the gurney, covered her up with heated blankets, and rolled her to the patient room where Emmy's teammates and their wives waited for her.

When they opened the door to the room, they each stood and waited as he and Quinn parked the gurney in the middle of the far wall, plugged in the monitors to watch her heart, lungs, and temperature.

He turned to look at each of them as Quinn fussed a bit and added to Emmy's chart. "She did well. No adverse reaction to the serum. She'll wake in a few minutes and after she wakes completely, we'll see if she can tolerate some soup and if she does, we'll bring her home to recuperate."

33

She woke to the voices of her friends softly chatting and reliving their adventure from last night. She heard Casper's name a couple of times and became a bit more alert wanting to know what Casper had said. She felt groggy and tried rubbing her eyes.

Chase's voice was close, and his hands took hers and pulled them away from her eyes but held them in his. "Don't rub your eyes, Emmy. They'll feel dry for a bit and maybe a little gritty, but it's important you don't rub them right now. Okay?"

"Yes."

Her mouth was dry and she tried moving her tongue around to find moisture. "Thirsty."

"I'll let you chew some ice chips, but we need to wait until all the anesthesia is out of your system before you drink anything. It might hit your stomach hard."

Kori stepped forward with a cup of ice from the bedside table and handed it to him. He slid his left hand under Emmy's head and gently lifted her, then touched the cup to her lips and tilted it so she could take in a couple of ice chips.

He pulled it away and she chewed on the ice. "Just a little more please."

He tilted the cup again and let her have a couple more chips. "That's all for now. I'm sorry."

His words rattled around in her brain. "I'm sorry." The first time he'd said that to her he'd told her he was engaged to someone else and her heart broke. Now, it didn't break her heart and as he lowered her head to the pillow gently, she wondered about that.

"Emmy, how is your pain? On a scale of one to ten, with ten being the worst pain, where are you?"

She opened her eyes and looked into his. She blinked several times to moisten them. And each time her eyelids opened, his beautiful hazel eyes stared at her. She loved looking at his eyes. She loved seeing them the first thing every morning. The past couple of mornings had been wonderful in that she saw him first each day. And last each night. When she wasn't wracked with pain, she allowed herself to feel happy about that. Even if she didn't know where it would lead. Even if she left him here once she could travel home and never saw him again, she'd take those memories with her. But the thought of leaving him here nearly pulled the breath from her lungs.

Her heartbeat sped up and he asked again. "Emmy, on a scale of one to ten..."

"I heard. I needed to think about it a minute. To be honest, my pain isn't bad. Not as bad as it had been before. I'd say about a five."

"That's fantastic. It should improve from there."

She inhaled a deep breath and looked at her teammates sitting around the room staring at her. "Tell me what Casper said."

Chase chuckled and turned to look at her teammates. Falcon stood and neared her bed. "He called to say Smith is secured and so are Tito Hogan and Travis Preston. Though none of them are cooperating. Casper also wanted you to know they have Smith's phone and are putting a tracking map together to line up the kidnapping of Piper and the women we found on the boat." He glanced briefly at Hope and she nodded. "And the women at the warehouse. The Russian women we found in Las Vegas are speaking with Casper's liaisons and offering dates and names. Casper will try to match up payments to those men from Smith or SmithCo. He'll keep us informed."

"Okay." She felt elated that they'd stopped Smith. Her heart felt light and happy. They'd done what they set out to do. "Also, your parents are on their way here."

Her eyes flew open. "What?" The heart monitor beeped faster as she looked at Falcon. "Why?"

"Em, you know GHOST was watching with Cyber as Smith was taken down. Your Uncle Gaige called Auggie and Dane and they wanted to talk to you. After many questions, Gaige told them you had surgery."

She inhaled a deep breath. "Fuck."

Falcon laughed and so did Chase. "I'm sure once they see you're fine they'll be less pissed and more grateful. But, you know, parents, right?"

She let out a long breath. "Right."

She tried sitting up and Chase held her shoulders down. "Hold on, you might be dizzy from the anesthesia."

"I have to get out of here. Chase, what you did for me is amazing, but my dad has connections, and you basically stole from the military. This can be bad."

"I told you I did what I thought was right. They had this serum at Walter Reed when you were there. They neglected to use it on you, a prime candidate. How will they explain that to anyone higher up? Unless the whole military is involved in selling off medical experimentation for profit."

Quinn entered the room with a tray in her hands. A steaming bowl of soup, crackers, and a bottle of water rested on the tray. She set it on the bedside table and the aroma of chicken noodle soup teased her nostrils and her stomach growled.

Chase laughed. "See, you're hungry, that's wonderful."

Quinn pulled the tray table to the bed and Chase raised her head with the bed's remote. "How is your hip handling the movement?"

"Fine. I feel a slight pulling where I assume I have stitches, but nothing bad."

She saw Chase glance at Quinn with a slight smile on his handsome face, but she let it go. She didn't want to sound like a jealous woman. Plus, she wasn't sure what she felt right now was jealousy. More curious about that smile.

She picked up her spoon and sipped in some of the warm soup. She could feel the warmth travel down her throat and though it seemed like canned soup, it was tasty enough that she wanted more. As she ate, she noticed the room was quiet. She looked at her teammates and shrugged. "You're going to sit there and watch me like I'm an animal in the zoo?"

Kori laughed. "No. We're just happy to see your face look so peaceful. The past few weeks you've looked positively miserable. You don't now."

She stopped the spoon halfway to her mouth and stared at Kori. "Really?"

"Really."

She hadn't realized it. She'd been in pain for years, the past few weeks were absolutely miserable, but she'd been patting herself on the back because she kept going. She had a company to run and a criminal empire to topple. Slowing down didn't seem an option to her.

Her phone rang from Kori's pocket and Kori pulled it out and looked at the screen. She grimaced slightly. "It's your mom."

34

He settled Emmy in bed, no need for ice packs now, just let her rest until the anesthesia moved from her system. Dane and Keirnan were on their way to the house after checking into their hotel room and he was nervous. He wasn't sure what she'd told them about him if she'd ever said anything at all. And the last thing he wanted was either of her parents mad at him. That's not a great way to start out. At least he hoped this was a new start.

Falcon and Kori were making supper for everyone. Creed and Hope took a walk and Diego and Ted were upstairs talking to Shelby and the kids. At least Diego was talking, but Ted barked once or twice, so he was communicating in his own way. Chase wearily sat on the sofa and stared off into space.

Kori looked up at him. "Hey, why don't you go and take a nap? Emmy's sleeping and you look like you haven't slept in days."

"What about when Dane and Keirnan get here?"

Falcon shrugged, "We'll let you know."

"But won't they be..."

Falcon laughed. "Go fucking take a nap."

Chase nodded and pulled his weary body to his full height and quietly crept into the bedroom where Emmy slept. He gently laid down on his side of the bed and rolled to his side to watch her sleep. She was incredible, even in sleep. Though her stature was fairly small. Small framed, only five foot two in height, she was a powerhouse for sure. Her convictions were deep, her honor strong as steel and her love was what he wanted most in this world. He'd known it from the first moment he met her. When he'd stopped following her career, he told himself she was too good for him, and he needed to let her move on. He needed to move on. But, neither of them did. That says a lot right there.

Her right hand was between them and he laid his left hand over it, absorbing her heat. The softness of her skin. His heavy eyes closed, and he was lulled to sleep by Emmy's deep even breaths.

He felt the bed dip and opened his eyes. By the looks of the height of the sun he'd slept around an hour but what struck him the most was Emmy was sitting on the edge of the bed, her feet on the floor and she brushed her hand back and forth over her incision.

"Are you in pain?"

She turned her head to look at him over her shoulder, her long dark hair swaying as she did. "No. It's amazing."

He jumped up and walked around the bed to her and knelt down in front of her. He put his hand over the incision. It wasn't warm. His hand moved to her forehead and her neck and there was no fever. Her eyes were clear and bright and her lips parted into the most beautiful smile he'd ever seen. "I don't have pain, Chase."

He stood and held his hands out to her. She placed her hands in his and stood. It was effortless and graceful. Their eyes locked together, and she stepped forward and kissed his lips.

Instantly his arms wrapped around her body, her waist, and her shoulders and he pulled her in tightly until there was no space between them. Her arms circled his waist and his lips commanded hers.

Her full lips fit his like they were made for each other. His tongue slid into her mouth and swirled around, and she moaned. He felt it deep in her chest where they were pressed together. Their kisses had always been spectacular, but not like this. They enjoyed each other for long moments at a time, then pulled back for air only to seek each other's lips once more.

"Em?"

"No. Don't say anything."

"But..."

Voices could be heard in the living room and she turned her head. "My parents are here."

Dane's voice then said, "What do you mean they're sleeping together?"

"Yep. Definitely here." She smiled, kissed him once more, then tugged on his hand. "Let's go see my parents."

He watched her walk, besides enjoying the view, she had no discernible limp, no indication that she'd ever had a serious injury. It was remarkable. "Em, you're walking. It's amazing."

She laughed. "I haven't felt this good in years. Still just a small tingling and maybe some itching, but other than that, the pain is gone."

She held her hand out to him and he stepped to her and took it in his. They clasped fingers together as they walked out of the bedroom and all voices ceased to speak as they entered the living room together.

She dropped his hand and walked to the older woman in the room and pulled her in for a long hug. She turned then and hugged her father then took a couple steps back and slowly turned around as everyone watched in amazement.

"I can walk again. Pain-free. I can walk again pain free and it's fantastic."

Chase's mind swirled around. They'd never had such immediate results as this in any of their test patients. He'd call Karol as soon as he could tonight. What had she said when she gave this to him? "Third generation." That was it. Third generation. They've been improving it. Making it work faster.

"Chase?"

He blinked and took a deep breath. Emmy stood staring at him. "Chase, this is my father, Dane, and my mother, Keirnan. Mom and Dad, this is Chase Nicholas."

He stepped forward and shook her father's hand then Keirnan wrapped her arms around him and squeezed him tight. "Thank you for helping Emmy."

He whispered. "It was my pleasure."

Creed finally said, "Holy shit, Em. I can't believe my eyes."

She giggled. "I know. I can't believe it either."

Diego asked, "How long is that going to last?"

He didn't know about this third generation. The first and second generations that he'd worked on hadn't met their end dates yet. Did the third gen? Another thing he'd have to ask Karol.

"I honestly don't know."

The others excitedly chattered on about Emmy's remarkable progress and he could only think about calling Karol. This was remarkable. No one had ever had such incredible progress.

35

Emmy sat on the deck outside in a rocking chair and watched two squirrels play. They jumped from branch to branch, chittered and scurried then ran off to another branch to do it all again. All she really wanted to do was take a walk or hike in the woods or do something active, she'd been rather dormant for years now. But her parents had asked her to take it easy and Chase whispered in her ear, "I need to call Karol and talk to her about this. I've never seen anyone recover this fast. Please stick close until I can speak with her."

She smiled at him and nodded. Then, puzzled about her feelings on everything, she came out here to sit while everyone else cleaned up after supper. Chase went to the bedroom to call Karol and she sat here now wondering what to do moving forward.

She is RAPTOR. She can't just up and move. Not that they'd even hinted at anything more serious. She had changed since she was with him last. More of an edge. Sharper in her focus and married to her work. Back when she and Chase had been together, she didn't have her eyes on a career other than the military and going back to work at GHOST. But nothing was set in stone. She hadn't spoken to Uncle Gaige about working at GHOST, she just always knew she could if she wanted. But, somewhere in the far reaches of her mind, she now realized she hadn't set things in stone because she was waiting to see what would happen with Chase. She'd go with him wherever he went. It was hard to admit that to herself now, but as she thought about it right now, she knew it was true.

So, when someone says things happen for a reason, she believed it with her whole heart. She was an independent, strong woman and she would have allowed herself to go without question and never have a solid career because they might have to move to another base in a couple of years. That was the part of her that was like her mom. Not her biological mom, but Keirnan, the only mom she'd ever known. She was strong in a soft way. Her dad always teased her mom, "You're an iron hand in a velvet glove Keirnan." She'd be strong wherever her family was.

The door opened and her mom stepped outside. "Mind if I sit with you?"

"Not at all."

Her mom pulled the second rocking chair on the deck next to her and sat.

"How are you feeling?"

"I feel good, Mom. Amazing actually."

Her mom reached over and held her hand as they rocked together.

"What are you thinking about?"

"Life." She turned her head and looked at her mom. She was a beautiful woman. While there were fine lines around her eyes and her mouth, her skin was still clear and soft, her eyes were sharp and missed very little.

"Life. That's a big subject."

She chuckled. "It sure is."

"Does this life include Chase?"

She turned her head back to the squirrels and rested the back of her head against the chair. "I don't know."

Her mom said nothing and they rocked in unison for a while.

"How long have you known him?"

"Years. We were on base together before I went to Afghanistan."

"Ah. That makes sense then."

"Makes sense about what?"

"He looks at you differently than he looks at others. There's a familiarity between you two that doesn't happen in a few days."

She thought about how much to tell her mom and decided to keep the ugly stuff away. At least for now. She had a hard enough time figuring out everything as it was.

"When did you get back in touch?"

She giggled slightly. "When I came here. I was out on a mission with Falcon, Creed, and Diego when my hip snapped. They took me to the hospital, and it turned out Chase was working. Also, Kori has been friends with Chase for years and kept asking me to see him to help me. But she never told me his name and I never asked. So, it's been a weird set of circumstances."

Her mom chuckled. "Everything happens for a reason."

Giggling she looked over at her mom. "I was just thinking that before you came out here."

Her mom smiled and watched the squirrels for a moment. "What will you do when you leave here?"

She let out a long breath. "I don't know."

They rocked for a while then her mom asked, "What do you want to happen?"

"I don't know." She stopped rocking and leaned forward, elbows on her knees. "I can't leave RAPTOR. I won't. We haven't talked about anything. It's still so new again. But, in a weird way, like we've never been apart. He hurt me when we were on base. That's why I took the post in Afghanistan. I ran away when I should have stayed and fought. He said he followed my career for a while then decided to let me go. He didn't fight either. So, I'm confused about what that means. Are my feelings left over from last time? Or are these feelings real and have simply been lying dormant all these years?"

Her mom took a deep breath and leaned over and rubbed her back.

"When I met your father, I thought he was the most handsome man I'd ever met. He had you and I saw what a great father he was. You were a source of sunshine every day in class, and I was drawn to you in ways I couldn't explain. My other students, well, I loved them all, but I loved you a bit more. I wasn't looking for a relationship at the time. Neither was he. Newly out of the service and figuring out what he was going to do with his life. But, almost from the beginning, something we both felt so strongly about was that when either of us thought of our future, we didn't see a future without the other in it. So, I ask you, when you close your eyes and think of the future, is Chase there?"

36

Chase hung up the phone and heaved out a big sigh. He wished he'd known some of this before he'd used the serum on Emmy. Informed consent is essential. But Karol didn't think it was a big deal and she didn't have the time to explain it as she was being immediately transferred.

He stepped into the living room and saw Diego texting on his phone.

"Hey, Emmy and Keirnan are out on the deck." He nodded with his head.

"Okay. Where's Dane?" He may as well tell them all at the same time.

"In the garage with Falcon."

Turning to see Keirnan and Emmy rocking, he decided to see what they were discussing and let them make the call whether to include Dane.

The moment he stepped onto the deck several things hit him. The humidity was high and his skin instantly felt damp. The wildlife was having a grand old time and making noise and Emmy looked peaceful. So did Keirnan.

Emmy turned her head but didn't lift it from the back of the chair. "Hey."

"Hey."

"Did you speak with Karol?"

"Yeah." He swallowed to moisten his throat and his heart flipped in his chest. God, he didn't want to let her down.

She pointed to a chair across from her and smiled. "Well, sit and tell us all about it."

He glanced at Keirnan and noticed her serene smile. Her shoulders were relaxed and then he saw their hands clasped together.

"I didn't mean to interrupt. I can come back later."

Emmy scoffed. "Nope. Sit. Tell us."

Hesitating only minutely, he strode forward and took the plastic chair at the table, and pulled it in front of their rocking chairs. He leaned down and placed his elbows on his knees then found that uncomfortable and sat up straight.

Emmy stopped rocking and sat up straight. "Now you're just starting to scare me."

"It's not bad. At least as of now, it isn't." He crossed his left ankle over his right knee. "Do you want your dad out here for this conversation?"

Em shook her head. “We can tell him later.”

“The serum Karol gave me was third generation. She told me that and we were so rushed and worried about being caught, she didn't expand on it, and I didn't ask. It never occurred to me she'd offer something that hadn't been tested. At least not appropriately tested."

"Okay."

Keirnan stopped rocking and sat up straighter now as well.

“Typically, we'd want enough test subjects to collect data on. What works for one person doesn't always work for another and so on. Diet, environment, physical stature, family health history and so much more comes into play. We were working with one thousand test subjects on generation one." He swallowed. "Generation two had only a couple of hundred and they were pushing her so fast that generation three has only had a dozen or so test subjects. That isn't enough to really know what this will do."

Emmy cocked her head. "Why were they pushing her so hard?"

"Speed. They wanted the serum to work faster. The second generation doubled the speed. This generation, the third, tripled it. You recovered in hours.

"That's why they sold it off. They can get athletes back on the football or baseball or whatever field in hours.

"They were pushing for more. Faster. They wanted to be able to take an injured football player, inject him and have him back on the field in a few minutes."

Emmy sat back in her chair. "Holy shit."

Keirnan finally said. "They must have made a fortune."

"I'm sure they did. And Karol's resistance to pushing faster without facts put her on a list. When she balked at selling it off, they pulled her off completely. I bet there's a secret lab somewhere still testing military personnel. The civilian lab wouldn't have the knowledge and the people in the military selling this off would be stupid to give up the formula. Karol said she saw things being packed up as she left the lab. In case she told someone or plans to, it would be gone before anyone got there to see it and she'd be deemed unreliable."

Emmy took a deep breath. "So, your concern right now is you don't know if there will be side effects for me?"

"Yes." He swiped his hands down his face and took a deep breath. "We don't know. What if your organs object to the rapid change? What if it affects brain activity or causes organ failure?"

"What if it doesn't do anything?"

"That is the best possible outcome, Em. But we'll have to be very diligent and catalog everything as you move forward in the next year. Years even."

"So, I'm a test subject?"

He leaned forward and took her hands in his. "I don't want you to feel that way, but I am worried about this. I don't want anything to happen to you."

Emmy stared at him for a long time. He could smell her fresh scent as a light breeze blew through her hair. She turned and looked at her mom. "What do you think?"

Keirnan smiled softly. "I don't think you have a choice. He can't take the serum out."

"I don't want that. This is the first day in years I haven't had pain."

"And, since he only wants to make sure you don't have issues moving forward, what's the harm?"

"It feels like an invasion of privacy."

He shook his head. "I won't share your information with anyone else. Since legally, I'm not supposed to have the serum." His eyes darted to Keirnan.

He continued, "I have nowhere to upload your data or do anything with it other than keep it for myself."

She licked her lips and sighed. "I guess I don't have a choice."

He chuckled then. "You're the one who is all about helping others who can't help themselves. Instead of resisting this, I thought you'd be more open to it."

Her eyes bored into his for a long time and she bit her lip once more. "Did you know about this before you used the serum on me? Be honest with me. Not like last time."

Keirnan asked, "What last time?"

Chase slowly shook his head. "When Emmy and I broke up, it was because I had lied to her about being engaged to someone else. A girl back home. The engagement was a mistake and I should never have entered into a relationship with Emmy before breaking it off. I was in the wrong."

Keirnan swallowed and stared at him. "Well, it appears you've learned a hard lesson."

"That I have."

Emmy huffed out a breath. "What did Karol find out about Walter Reed?"

"It's pathetic. They didn't want to try it on you because they already had more than one hundred test patients with a similar injury. By that time, they were only selecting patients with injuries they hadn't tested the serum on. That's all she could see in the computer. Neither of us were there, so actual conversations are lost on us."

37

Emmy pulled her long hair back and up and twisted a rubber band around it to make a ponytail on top of her head. It felt good to have her hair off her neck. Since she'd come in from outside, the humidity had hung on her like a cloak.

The tingling in her hip had somewhat subsided and it didn't hurt when it was there, it was just a reminder. After this meeting, she'd change her bandage and see how her incision looked. Overall, she felt fantastic. Any small amount of pain seemed like nothing at all compared to what she was used to.

She looked around the room at her teammates, her parents, and Chase ready to discuss a few things.

"So, first of all, let's pack up and head home in the morning."

Cheers went up around the room. Except for Chase and that twisted her stomach.

"Therese will be here at eight so we'll need to run through the checkout list and be out of here no later than seven. Mom and Dad, I assume you're planning on joining us?"

Her father nodded, then looked at her mom, then nodded again. "Yes, and thank you."

She swallowed. "I have a follow-up call with Casper scheduled for tomorrow afternoon. Anyone available should be there so you can hear first-hand what his update is. GHOST team members will be there as well. Any questions?"

Heads shook and no one said a thing. "Okay, thanks, everyone. Once again, great job."

As quickly as they could all leave, they did. There was packing to do, and they were eager to get home, especially Diego.

Her parents stood and stepped up to her. Her mom hugged her first. "I love you Emmy and I'm so proud of you. I'll see you in the morning." She leaned in close and whispered in her ear. "You need to think hard about what you'll do concerning Chase."

"I know, Mom."

Her dad stepped into her outstretched arms and hugged her close. "I love you Emmy girl. I am so darned proud of you too. You're a kick-ass operative, team leader, and daughter."

She chuckled. "Thanks, Dad. You're pretty kick-ass too. Dad, operative, sounding board, mentor, and dad."

"You said dad twice."

"I meant to."

Her father kissed her forehead and stepped away. He turned and strode to Chase and held his hand out. Chase shook her father's hand and nodded.

Her dad brought tears to her eyes when he said, "Thank you for helping my little girl. It killed us seeing her in so much pain. I can't tell you what it feels like to see her standing here without the visages of pain on her face. I'll never be able to thank you enough."

Chase swallowed and nodded but said nothing, and she saw his eyes well with emotion.

Her mom stepped up to Chase and hugged him. She whispered something but Emmy couldn't hear it. She wondered what was said but decided not to dwell on it.

Her parents walked out the front door with a wave goobye and Emmy smiled and waved in return. She turned to Chase. "Maybe we should talk."

"Yes."

Chase passed her and locked the door leading to the deck, then hurried around and locked the front door and the garage door. She watched him briefly, then went into the bedroom.

Chase followed her in and quietly closed the door. She turned to face him and looked into his eyes. His were filled with worry but were still those beautiful, lash-framed eyes she loved to look at. He took a step forward and raised his right hand and laid it on her cheek. His thumb swiped gently over her bottom lip and she pursed her lips and kissed it.

That caused him to pull away and straighten his posture.

"You never pulled away from my kisses before."

"I know this sounds hypocritical, but I don't want to lose my heart."

"You're right, it does."

"So, this is goodbye?"

She took a deep breath and stared at him longer. "What do you want it to be Chase?"

"I want it to be hello." He swallowed. "I want to spend time with you. I want to make a life with you. I wanted it before and I know I handled it all wrong. Believe me, I..."

He scraped his hand through his hair and sucked in a deep breath. "If I could change one thing in my life, it would be that I'd never proposed out of a sense of duty and guilt. I would have been free to pursue what we started all those years ago. I would change that."

A tingle raced through her body so much different than the tingling she'd been feeling in her hip. It was a spark of electricity that generated speed as it moved faster and faster. It swept through her vital organs first then gathered speed and zinged through her muscles and tummy, quickly energizing between her legs and zipped back up her body and smashed into her heart. Her heart responded by thudding loudly and quickly as she watched his face waiting for him to douse the flames by saying something stupid, like it had been the right thing to do.

He opened his mouth and what came out nearly dropped her to her knees.

"I loved you then Emersyn Copeland. I've loved you all the years since from afar. I love you now in a mature, responsible, sensual manner. I love you, Em."

She took a shaky breath, afraid to move. To break the spell that just wrapped itself around her. He loved her.

When she spoke, it was a whisper. "How can you know that?"

"I know I've longed for you all these years. I know when I first saw you again a few days ago it was as if I was in shock. My knees shook, my mind couldn't wrap itself around the fact that you're here. But I also knew I would do anything to not lose touch with you again. Not unless you tell me you don't have feelings for me."

Her mom's words came back to her mind in a whoosh. *When you look into the future, do you see Chase in it?* She swallowed the cottony ball that formed in her throat and forced her breathing to even out. This was the moment she'd remember for the rest of her life.

38

His heart felt like it would leap out of his chest. She stared at him for so long, saying nothing that he began to dread what would come next. She didn't want him in her life. If she loved him too, she'd have jumped into his arms, wouldn't she?

She inhaled a breath so deep it lifted her shoulders.

"I love you too." She said it softly and he almost asked her to repeat it.

"You love me? You hesitated so long I thought..."

Shaking her head stopped him. "Yes. I love you. I always have. I was so pissed when I saw you a few days ago, mostly because you made me feel again. You made my heart race. My skin prickled with desire to touch you. My fingers itched to touch you and it pissed me off that I still felt that way after all this time. After you broke my heart."

"I'm so sorry Em. Honestly, if I could change it..."

"I know."

He stepped closer and wrapped his arms around her waist and pulled her close. His lips found hers and when they touched, emotions flew through his body like a raging fire. Their tongues danced to their own rhythm, they held tightly to each other and his mind struggled to catch up.

She pulled at his shirt, tugging it from his jeans. She started pulling it up over his head, but he halted her.

"Hey. Let's...We need to slow down. Let me look at your incision to make sure everything is alright."

She giggled, "You want to play doctor with me?"

He chuckled. "Well, yeah, I do. But first, I want to be the doctor and make sure we don't do any damage to your hip."

She sighed and nodded. "Okay. Doctor. What do you want me to do?"

"As sexy as you are in those yoga pants, please take them off."

She giggled and it was like music. She backed up until her legs touched the bed, then she shimmied her yoga pants over her slender hips and pushed them down her legs. He grinned at her playfulness, oh how he'd missed it. Her. He'd missed her.

"Okay. Lay down and let me look at your incision."

She wrinkled her nose. "That's not terribly sexy Chase."

"I know. But it's important. The most important thing I can do for you right now is make sure we don't do anything to cause a setback. Please know, I'd love nothing more than to ignore all of this, but, you know, first, do no harm and all that."

She smiled. "I admire your oath and I'll behave. For now."

She laid back on the bed and turned on her side, showing him her fine derriere. She wore a black thong, and he spent a moment admiring her, then she turned her head to look at him over her shoulder, a sexy grin on her face. "I thought you were in doctor mode."

"That doesn't mean I'm not a man." He stepped forward and softly brushed his fingers over her exposed butt cheeks. "You're sexy Em. Damn sexy."

She chuckled. He gently lifted the corners of the medical tape holding the gauze over her incision then slowly peeled the bandage back. He froze as he looked at her incision, bewildered at what he was seeing. His fingers gently touched the skin around her incision then softly brushed down the stitches.

"Why are your brows furrowed?"

She lifted up and looked at her hip, then her brows bunched together. "Where did it go?"

"I don't know."

"You've never seen this before?"

"No." He pulled his phone from his pocket. "May I take a picture? I want to send it to Karol and ask her if this is normal."

She swallowed and bit her bottom lip. Then she nodded. "Okay."

"It's research Em. Do you know what we could be on to here? It doesn't matter. Karol and I are planning on recreating it in our own lab and using it on veterans, police, fire, and EMTs. We can help them. Save their lives."

"Didn't you sign a non-compete?"

"I did for the first generation. Not this one."

"How will you recreate it?"

He tugged her shoulder so she laid back on the bed and he could look her in the eye. "We procured a couple of samples. Between my knowledge of what we did and hers, and the samples we can dissect, we can recreate this."

Emmy swallowed and he worried. "I didn't lie to you. I wasn't sure where we were going. If you even wanted to be with me. But we love each other. We can change the world in our respective careers Em. You're saving trafficking victims and putting traffickers behind bars and I can heal our wounded brothers and sisters in arms."

"Where? Where will your lab be?"

He shrugged. "I don't know. Karol has eight months on her contract with the Army. We didn't talk specifics, just that we could do this. And there isn't any reason we can't work independently and compare our testing and formulas."

"It can take years to set up a lab. At least if it's to be a secret."

He nodded. "I know. But, in the meantime, I'll still have my medical practice and can work on the formula on the side. Most of it is a lot of waiting for things to cure anyway."

"So you want to stay here?"

She sat up and hugged her knees and warning bells went off in his brain.

"I never said that."

"You said you'd have your practice."

"I can practice medicine anywhere."

"I can't stay here. I am RAPTOR. It's my business and I have to go back to Lynyrd Station."

He sat in front of her and gently pulled her hands apart and held them in his. Ducking his head down slightly so they were eye to eye he smiled at her. "I love you, Emersyn Copeland. I am in love with you. I have been for years. I'll go wherever you are."

39

Looking into his eyes she knew he was honest. He was worried and she didn't want that. But...

"Chase, you have to be sure. This is big."

"It's big. And you are the best of it. If you aren't in my life, I'll still work in a lab somewhere in my spare time. But I won't be happy. I'll still be a doctor, but I'll be a shell of a man. Knowing the only woman in the world for me is somewhere else, maybe with someone else."

His eyes never left hers and she was without a doubt sure, she didn't see her future without Chase in it.

She leaned forward and kissed his soft lips. They were warm and comforting and inviting and she wanted to kiss him forever. His hand rested on the side of her face, and she cupped his head in her hands. He leaned forward and set his phone on the bedside table.

She pulled back. "I thought you wanted a picture."

"Not if it makes you uncomfortable."

"But it's important for your research."

"You're more important for my life."

She sighed. "Take your picture, then make love to me."

He cocked his head and looked at her for a moment. She nodded and smiled, then rolled to her side, exposing the stitches that were holding nothing together. Only a faint line showed where just this morning he'd used a scalpel and made an incision.

He grabbed his phone and snapped three pictures. One up close to the stitches. The second a bit further away. He reached over and pulled her shirt down so her waist wasn't showing and snapped the third photo standing up straight.

He looked at them, then showed her. "This is what I'm sending to Karol."

She scrolled through the pictures. "It isn't even red."

"I know."

"It's so weird."

"I know."

"Can you take them out?"

He nodded then stepped into the closet and came out with his medical bag and set it on the bed. Moving into the bathroom, he came out with two towels and set them next to her. He had simple tools in his bag, a tweezers, scissors, and basic first aid supplies. He snapped a pair of rubber gloves on his hands and snipped the first stitch, then tugged it out. She barely felt it. He repeated the motions with each of the stitches and dabbed on antibiotic ointment and band-aids over the area to protect it. But the way she was healing, they'd be off tomorrow. It was a miracle.

She rolled to her back as he put his bag in the closet and when he stepped back into the room, she held her arms out to him, a sexy smile on her lips.

He approached the bed and she held up her hands. "Shirt and pants off please."

"You should practice what you preach."

She giggled and pulled her t-shirt over her head. Reaching back she unsnapped her bra and slid it off and dropped it to the floor. His shirt met her bra on the floor and his pants lay on top of the clothing pile. Emmy hooked her thumbs into her panties.

"I'll do that."

He tugged her panties down her hips and legs then kissed his way up her legs, stopping where her curls started. He grinned at her then slid his tongue along the seam of her pussy. She groaned and he did it again, so did she. Parting her lips with his tongue, he sucked her clit into his mouth and flicked it with his tongue.

"Chase." She hissed out. Oh, my gawd. It had been so long. So, long. His tongue was amazing.

He repeated his previous ministrations, then slowly slid his forefinger into her wetness. His fingers were smooth, which normally would have bothered her. She worked with men who had work-roughened hands and hers were slightly rough too. Handling guns, and ammo and working out, in general, made a person's hands a bit coarse. But she loved how Chase's hands felt on her.

He sucked her clit into his mouth and moved his finger in and out in time with his lips and she felt the flush crawl up her body, her skin dampened, and her body felt on fire. Her orgasm hit her fast and hard and if she weren't lying down, she'd have fallen for sure. Her legs shook from its intensity.

He licked her a few times as she came back to earth, then kissed his way up her torso, suckling her breasts, then kissing her lips.

"You taste amazing."

Her eyes opened slowly and he grinned. "You're sexy like this Em. Relaxed, sated, and wanton."

She sighed.

He whispered, "I'm clean."

"Me too."

"I don't have a condom."

"If we're both clean, we don't need it."

His knees spread her legs wider. She lifted them and hooked her ankles around his butt. He stopped momentarily and looked at her hip, then back to her and smiled. Slowly, so incredibly slowly, he entered her and inch by inch she felt so complete. She'd been missing him so much more than she thought. Her emotions had been so riled up these past few days and she loved that she'd finally settled into forgiveness and allowed herself to love him again. It was so much better than not.

He pulled out and pushed back in and she opened her eyes and saw him watching her.

He grinned, "I missed you."

"I missed you too."

Out and back in. They fell into the dance of the ages as they each sought to bring the other pleasure. His dance began to speed up and she matched him movement for movement. Then he pushed into her hard a couple of times and she orgasmed again. "Thank fuck," he mumbled just as he spilled himself into her.

He held himself off of her slightly with his arms, but she could feel his heartbeat and it was as rapid as hers. Her arms circled around his back, and she lazily brushed her hands up and down his back, enjoying the warmth of his skin against her hands.

She drifted off to a blissful sleep shortly afterward.

40

Chase walked into the bathroom as Emmy brushed her teeth. He held his phone in front of her so she could read Karol's text.

"Tell Emmy congratulations. I'm thrilled she's recovered so quickly. We had one other patient recover at that pace and so far, four months later, she's doing splendidly."

Emmy spit her toothpaste into the sink and rinsed, then turned and wrapped her arms around his shoulders. "Thank you for letting me read that."

"Of course."

She kissed his lips, then turned and tucked her toothbrush into its travel holder and then put the holder and toothpaste into her toiletry bag.

"When are you coming to Lynyrd Station?"

"How about Saturday?"

"And how long will you stay?"

He shrugged. "Forever?"

She laughed and carried her toiletry bag into the bedroom and dropped it into her duffle bag. She pulled her brush out of her duffle bag and pulled her long hair over her shoulder. Running the brush through her long strands he watched mesmerized. "I'll give notice at the hospital today. I'll have to step it up and do double duty at the clinic to see all the patients I can. I'll talk to Isaac and see if he wants the clinic before I tell my landlord I'll be leaving. He's mentioned a couple of times that he'd like his own clinic."

She swept her glossy hair over her shoulder and looked at him. "If this is too much, too fast, I understand."

He pulled her into his arms and kissed her forehead. "I can't get there fast enough to start our lives together. Promise."

"Okay. We'll be having a party on Saturday for all the celebrations we've missed while out on this mission, so if you need me to send the plane, I can do that."

He laughed. "I don't know that I'll get used to that. I've got it. If I can get there Friday night, I will so I won't be late."

"Okay." She looked around the room, then shrugged. "Okay, I'm all set."

He tried to smile, but he was going to miss the hell out of her the next few days. "Me too."

They each picked up their bags and exited the bedroom. Kori and Falcon were wiping down the counter and taking out the garbage. They both froze when they saw her.

Falcon spoke first. "Holy shit Em. You aren't limping at all."

"I know. Not only that, the incision healed and Chase took the stitches out last night."

Kori walked around the counter and stood in front of her. "Are you kidding?" Her eyes darted between the two of them.

Chase chuckled. "Not kidding. She's a miracle."

Diego and Ted came downstairs. Diego dropped his bag near the front door then looked at the coffee pot. "No coffee?"

Falcon shook his head. "We'll stop on the way and get something to eat and drink." He nodded toward Kori. "She'll need to hang her head out the window though. Morning sickness has kicked in."

Diego shrugged and stepped back. "I'm out of range back here." He whistled for Ted. "Come on boy, let's go load up."

Creed and Hope came down next and Creed nodded then stepped out behind Diego with their bags. Hope came toward her. "How do you feel this morning?"

Emmy laughed then hopped up and down a couple of times.

"No way!" Hope pulled her in for a hug and held tight for a few minutes. "That's wonderful."

Kori looked at him. "Chase. Will I see you again?"

He laughed and nodded. Then he put his arm around Emmy's shoulders and kissed the side of her head. "You will see me every day soon enough."

"That's fantastic." She clapped her hands together then hugged him briefly before hugging Emmy tightly. "I'm so happy for you."

He reached forward and shook Falcon's hand. "It's been a pleasure getting to know you, Falcon. I'll see you Saturday."

Falcon nodded then put his arm around Kori and ushered her to the front door.

Emmy turned to him and kissed his lips. "I'll see you Saturday."

"I can drive you to the airport."

She laughed. "It's out of your way. Let's keep it simple. I don't want to cry in front of everyone."

His heart instantly hurt. He thought he'd have more time with her. They'd just started over, he didn't want anything to get in the way of that. Last night he'd told her about Nicola, the biggest secret he'd carried in his life. She pulled him close and told him together, they'd fight these assholes, all of them.

He pulled her in tightly to his body and wrapped his arms securely around her. He kissed her temple then laid his head against hers. He could feel her heartbeat and it was strong. His beat faster at the moment and he enjoyed it.

She lifted her head and looked into his eyes. "I love you."

He smiled at her and nodded. "I love you too. See you Saturday, but every day we'll video conference."

"Yes, I look forward to that. Maybe we'll have video sex."

He chuckled then shrugged. "I've never done that."

"Me either." She giggled and he loved it.

Hand in hand they meandered to the door then stepped through it. It was as if the little sanctuary they'd had here evaporated. She pulled the door closed and pushed the button to lock it.

He leaned in and kissed her lips once more. Then he walked to his vehicle and she walked to hers. His truck was parked so it faced their SUV, and he watched Emmy step into the front passenger seat and buckle up. She didn't glance his way and his stomach soured. He would have scoffed at anyone who said he'd feel this way about her again. So fast. So strong. But it was like they'd never been apart. And this hurt more because they hadn't had the time to really solidify their relationship before parting again. Even if it was only four days, it felt heavy in his stomach.

Finally, she looked up and waved, and as he waved back his heart lifted. Diego drove them from the driveway and down the road and he followed until he had to turn in the opposite direction and head for the hospital. They'd speak tonight, but until then, he felt he'd be on pins and needles.

Taking a deep breath, he tapped the call button on his steering wheel. When the robotic voice asked him to say a command, he said, "Call Isaac."

41

Emmy walked into the conference room at RAPTOR headquarters and all heads turned to stare. She froze and cocked her head.

Piper was the first to speak. "Em. I don't think any of us have ever seen you walk without a limp. It's amazing and so hopeful for so many reasons."

"It is amazing." She smiled and relaxed. "It's mind-blowing actually. I'd almost forgotten how it felt to not be in pain every day. I'm still not used to it. Just getting out of the vehicle a bit ago my mind clenched up before I moved telling me it would hurt."

Piper sighed. "I'd love to know what it's like not to feel pain every day."

Emmy looked at her and cocked her head. Why couldn't the serum work on Piper? And Donovan's left eye was blind, would it bring his sight back? Caiden had lung damage, would it help him? Falcon's hearing was damaged, would it help him? It mended her. The questions flitted through her brain in rapid-fire succession, and she made a mental note to ask Chase what he thought before she said anything to the others. Unfortunately for the RAPTOR members who were amputees, it wouldn't grow back a limb, but there was always research moving forward where it could happen one day.

Emmy smiled at Piper as the phone on her desk rang. "That's Casper. Everyone ready?" She glanced around the room at the empty chairs and wondered where the GHOST team was.

She answered the phone sitting in the middle of the conference table. "Emersyn Copeland."

"Hello Emersyn, this is Casper. Is your team assembled?"

The door opened and the members of GHOST ambled in, along with her father. She smiled at them as they each took a seat at the conference table and responded. "Yes sir. All members of RAPTOR, Diego Josephs, Donovan Keach, Charlesia Bowers, Piper Roman, Caiden Marx, Deacon Smythe, Falcon Montgomery, and Creed Rowan are here. GHOST team members are Ford Montgomery, Lincoln Winters, Dodge and Jax Sager, Gaige Vickers, Hawk Delany, Wyatt Lawson, Axel Dunbar, Josh Masters, and my father, Dane Copeland, are present."

Casper laughed. "Very well represented indeed. Hello everyone and thank you for joining me on this call. First of all, Emersyn, congratulations to you and your team. What you have done is tremendous and we're just now getting the gist of all this particular group of criminals has done."

"Thank you, sir." Her cheeks heated and her father leaned across the table and squeezed her hand and winked at her. She smiled and inhaled deeply.

Casper continued. "Since Smith and SmithCo are so enormous, and Smith was quite mobile given his money, private planes, private yachts, holdings, and homes everywhere, we've managed to send troops into many of those homes and businesses and confiscate documents which are proving to be even more valuable than you'll ever know. We've only touched on the very tip of the iceberg, but we've managed to link Smith to the criminals we've previously arrested and have jailed and some we are looking for. Especially interesting and something I can't expound on, is his connection to not only Congressman Compton but another higher-up in the White House, which we're gathering evidence on as we speak. It's truly criminal how these people become so corrupt in office. Or perhaps they are corrupt before they get into office, but it certainly is a cesspool of gluttony, excess, and fraud."

"Casper, this is Dane Copeland."

"Hello, Dane. You must be proud of your little girl. I remember seeing pictures of her on Auggie's lap when she was five or six. He was a proud grandpa for sure."

"Yes, sir. We're all incredibly proud of her." Her father smiled at her.

"What can I do for you Dane?"

"Can you tell us whether you've ascertained that this group is indeed shut down?"

"At this time, because I do believe there are a few more of Smith's business partners on the street, I can absolutely say we've crippled them beyond functioning right now. Once we have all members under arrest and they begin turning on each other, I'll feel absolutely confident the operation will be shut down. But sadly, there is too much money involved in trafficking and until we ferret out all of them, it'll continue in some form or another."

Emmy's nose wrinkled but when she looked down the table at the men and women ready and willing to go out and find these assholes, her heart filled with pride.

She responded, "I'd like to say, in front of everyone in this room, that if you find something we can do to help, we want to be brought in on the case."

Heads nodded and a couple 'hell yeahs' were said and the smile that creased her face was so big it almost hurt.

"I will absolutely call you first before anyone else. We all know why GHOST was formed and how RAPTOR came to be, and sadly, there are too many times we need agencies such as yours. Both groups are at the top of my secret list."

"Thank you, sir."

"Ladies and gentlemen, thank you for a job well done. You should go to bed tonight and sleep easy because the number of women and children you've saved by pulling these people off the streets is innumerable and you have my gratitude."

She was surprised as her smile grew even larger. "Thank you, sir."

The others mumbled their thanks and Casper ended the call. "I'll let you all celebrate. Good day."

The line went dead and Emmy stood. "Let's have a drink or two!"

The noise level grew to the point her ears hurt. She was instantly wrapped in a hug by her father, "Where's Chase?"

"He'll be here Saturday."

"So what does that mean?"

She looked into his eyes. "We're together Dad. I don't know if Mom told you, but we dated years ago before I went to Afghanistan. We broke up, it was painful. For both of us. But we're moving forward. Let's just say, he's the one who didn't get away."

Her father threw his head back and laughed. "I love that." He hugged her again. "But I'll be watching. If he hurts you again, we're going to have issues, him and I."

She laughed into her father's chest. "Deal."

"Stop hogging her. I want to congratulate my niece."

She turned and her Uncle Gaige wrapped her in a warm embrace. "Congrats Emmy. You did good."

"I wouldn't have been able to do any of this without you and dad. Thank you for believing in me and helping me get RAPTOR started."

"I can't think of anyone who could have done better. Honestly. I'm proud of you. Sophie is too, she's dying to hug you, so brace yourself."

She laughed. "I can't wait."

She glanced at her father, then her Uncle Gaige. “Do you each have a couple of minutes to speak with me about a private matter?”

Her father’s brows drew close together and he sat down. Gaige nodded and sat and she reclaimed the chair she’d just vacated.

“It’s about Chase. He and Karol stole the serum from the military. He said if he were caught it would be worth it. I know it was wrong, but so is the Army for selling it off and not using it on our military. They could have sold it off and still used it for the purpose it was intended.”

Her dad nodded, “Em, two wrongs don’t make it right.”

“I know. We both know. But, I’d like to offer Chase a guarantee that neither of you will ever tell on him.”

Gaige sat back in his chair and looked at her father before turning to her. “I’d like to tell Casper and see if there isn’t something he can look into regarding the Superman project. Even if I don’t use Chase and Karol’s names, I’d like to let him know what’s happening so he can watch. At the very least, he may be able to get the serum used on the military as it had been prior.”

“How will you explain you found this out?”

“I don’t have a duty to tell all my secrets to Casper, just as he doesn’t to me. And, with the work we do for him, there are hundreds of ways we could have found this information out.”

42

Chase swallowed as he pulled up to the wrought iron gates in front of the large brick building. The place was beautifully landscaped, and the grounds were pretty. The home next to it looked like an old southern mansion perched on the corner lot and set on a hill. The two didn't go together aesthetically and yet they did somehow.

He pushed the button on the brick gate support.

"Name please." A voice asked.

"Chase Nicholas. Here for Emersyn Copeland."

The gates slid open and he slowly drove through.

He saw young children playing in the yard between the homes and people were all around in the yard playing various games. A group played bocce ball on one side of the yard, another played volleyball in another area. Music could be heard over speakers in the yard and laughter was everywhere. The weirdest thing was there weren't any cars visible. Where did all these people park?

He parked his truck in front of a bank of garage doors and looked around for the front door. He was flooded with doubt, anxiety, and fear. Once again, he was the new guy. He hated being the new guy.

Inhaling a deep breath he nabbed his phone from the cradle it rested in on his dash and opened the door to exit. A man approached him and he had to squint to see past the sun shining behind him.

Dane stopped just before him and held out his hand. "Glad you made it Chase. Emmy's a nervous wreck waiting for you."

"Thanks. I drove through the night to get here. Where is she?"

Dane smiled at him. "She's in the sideyard playing with the children. It's like she can't stop moving around and running again. She hasn't been pain-free in so long."

"I'm happy to hear that sir."

"You may as well call me Dane. My girl told me you two are together."

"Yes, si...Dane."

Dane turned and he quickly followed not sure if Dane was unhappy about he and Emersyn or not. His heart raced at the thought of seeing her. He'd thought about her non-stop for the past four days. Actually, it had been the past five years, but he wasn't going to dwell on that. She'd forgiven him, so he'd need to forgive himself one day.

A beautiful woman with long dark hair and a very round baby bump stepped onto the driveway just off the lawn near the bocce ball game unfolding. She smiled at Dane then turned toward him.

"Sophie, this is Dr. Chase Nicholas. Chase this is Gaige's wife, and my sister-in-law, Sophie."

He reached out and shook her hand. "Nice to meet you, Sophie."

"Thank you. I'm sorry it's brief, but I have to lie down for a bit. My back and legs are killing me."

"Of course, I'm sure we'll have time to talk later."

"You bet. See you later."

Sophie waddled away toward the southern mansion and Dane laughed. "There she is. Em, Chase is here." He yelled.

His eyes landed on her and his breathing staggered. She was laughing and skipping around a circle with a group of younger children. Her long dark hair floated in the breeze behind her. Her trim legs were encased in a sexy pair of jeans and molded to her ass perfectly. The fitted camouflage top she wore tucked perfectly into the jeans and showed off her beautiful shape. When she turned to look at him, her smile lit up the whole yard. She was undoubtedly the most beautiful woman he'd ever met. When her father called to her, she turned to see him and said something to the kids, then came running toward him. He quickly tucked his phone into his pocket and stepped forward to meet her. She jumped into his arms and he wrapped them around her and held her close to his body.

Her legs wrapped around his waist and her lips slammed onto his. They kissed briefly, but only because he knew everyone was watching and he felt self-conscious. He looked into her eyes and smiled. "You are so beautiful."

She laughed. "So are you."

It was his turn to laugh then she turned her head and smiled at her dad. "Thanks for bringing him back, Dad."

Dane laughed and shook his head. "You got it Emmy girl. Why don't you get Chase settled, I'll go find your mom."

He slowly set her down on the ground, then wrapped his arm around her shoulders.

She tilted her head up to him. "I was getting worried."

"You looked like you were having fun."

"Well, I was, but I was wondering when you'd get here."

"I drove all night, but then had a flat tire around ten this morning. By the time I got it changed, an hour had passed. So, it delayed me a bit. I'm sorry."

"Why didn't you let me know?"

"Honey, you've been planning this party all week. You told me every day how excited everyone was and I didn't want to worry you."

"Fair enough. Come on and let me show you where we live now."

He chuckled. "Okay."

They stopped at his truck and he pulled two suitcases from the back. He opened the passenger door and pulled his medical bag from the seat and Emmy reached for it. "I can help."

"Okay." He chuckled as he pulled his suitcases along behind him. He followed Emmy through a garage service door and saw all the vehicles inside. He laughed. "I wondered where all the cars were for all those people out there."

"This is only RAPTOR vehicles. GHOST has their own garage next door."

"Ah, the southern mansion?"

"Yep. It's underground over there. I'll ask Uncle Gaige to give you a tour. You've got to see that place, it's amazing."

Laughing he shook his head. "Okay."

They entered the main home through a door to the far left of the garage, toward the yard where Emmy played with the kids. The decor of the home was modern but not cold modern. The furnishings were of brown leather and warm tones, wooden tables, and beautiful art on the walls.

"So this is the living room. Everyone has their own in their apartments, but we also have this one in case someone is in the mood or in need of company."

"It's beautiful."

She smiled and turned. They walked across a foyer area which was small but decorated nicely with a small round table in the middle and a bouquet of fresh flowers in the middle of the granite top. An arched doorway led to a kitchen, where an older gentleman stood at the counter cutting up onions.

"Sheldon, this is Dr. Chase Nicholas. Chase, Sheldon is our chef. He's the best too."

Sheldon laughed and nodded. "Nice to meet you, doctor, I'd shake your hand, but you'll smell like an onion after, so let's hold off until later. Dinner will be ready in an hour."

"Sounds good Sheldon. Nice to meet you."

Emmy continued walking into a room on the other side of the kitchen. A large dining room was situated just behind the kitchen. A wall of windows looked out on the backyard and the children playing with rubber balls of varying colors was the main view at the moment. Squealing and laughing were heard above all else.

Emmy grinned. "Gosh, they're cute."

"That they are."

"So, we have to go back through to our room."

He stepped back and waited for her to pass him, then followed her dutifully. She nodded to Sheldon as she passed, and he grinned as the older gentleman continued slicing onions with a grin on his face.

In the foyer, she stopped and looked at him. "So, our apartments are in this wing." She pointed to a hallway opposite the living room. "Currently, Charly lives in her own home with her husband Sam. You'll meet everyone soon."

"I'll try to keep them all straight."

She laughed. "You won't forget Charly. Trust me."

She turned and started down the hallway. "Right now, Caiden, Deacon, and Falcon live down this hallway with us. Now that they're all married, we'll see if they stay or find their own homes." She pointed to each doorway as they passed them. "Our door is right here. The others live upstairs."

She used a card and swiped it in front of a keypad on the wall and the door locks opened.

Twisting the knob, she pushed the door open and stepped in. "This is our place."

He stepped into a small but pretty living room. The white leather sofa had a plush leopard print blanket draped across the far arm, and two animal print pillows graced either end of it. The dark wood coffee table in front of the sofa was a stark contrast and very eye-catching. The walls were painted a warm brown and the artwork on the walls was of various small-town settings. A television hung from the opposite wall and a white recliner sat to the left and at an angle to the sofa. Another plush blanket lay across the arm of it and he knew instantly that's where Emmy had spent a lot of time when she was in pain. His heart hurt for her once again.

"What do you think?"

"I think it's beautiful Em."

She smiled sweetly and pointed to an arched doorway. The white door stood open and he could see the corner of a bed. "This is our bedroom."

She stepped in before him and he looked around in awe. A large king-size bed stood in the middle of the far wall. A soft shiny brown, gold and tan comforter lay on top. The headboard was made of reclaimed wood and the dresser to the right matched it. The wall to his left was nearly an entire wall of closet. Barn doors hung from rungs to hide the clothing inside, but he knew what it was. She pointed to a doorway at the end of the closet. "That's our bathroom."

He stepped into the plush tile room, and walk-in shower, which he bet she had for her ease of use before the serum. "Emmy, this is fantastic."

She looked slightly nervous and he walked to her and pulled her in his arms.

She whispered. "I'm so glad you're here."

Her body shook slightly, and he pulled away and looked into her eyes. "Did you doubt me coming?"

"Yes."

His brows pinched together. "Why?"

She inhaled a deep breath and bit her bottom lip. "Insecurities, I guess. We went in different directions when I left. Just like last time."

"But we spoke every day. Several times."

"I know, but when it came right down to it, I wondered if you'd leave all you had built there for me."

"Oh, honey." He pulled her close again and inhaled the aroma of her hair. He closed his eyes and swallowed until the emotions settled. "I love you so much. The hardest thing in the world was letting you go with everyone else and me staying back there. I worried every minute of every day you'd decide you liked it here without me. But being an adult can be sucky and I had responsibilities. So did you."

"I know." She said it into his chest, and he stepped back.

Taking her hand in his, he laid her hand over his heart. "Do you feel that beating? How fast it's beating?"

"Yes."

"That's for you Em. All you. You captured my heart five years ago. I've never given it to anyone else. Not even a consideration. You've held it all these years."

She looked at their hands resting together over his heart for a long time. When she slowly lifted her eyes to his, he saw the moisture in them. Her soft lips turned up at the corners. "I've never given mine to anyone else either."

43

Emmy watched the groom kiss the bride and she swallowed to moisten her throat. Creed and Hope tied the knot in a beautiful little church her parents had joined that was on the outskirts of town. The sun shone through the stained-glass windows, making the whole church look like a kaleidoscope. Hope was simply beautiful, her slim body encased in a shiny but simple long gown. The train floated behind her and the colors from the windows glistened on her dress.

They turned to face the congregation and the minister introduced them. "Ladies and gentlemen, I'm pleased to introduce Mr. and Mrs. Rowan."

They clapped in unison and she watched Creed smile down at his wife. Both of them looked blissful.

Chase leaned down and whispered in her ear. "That was beautiful."

"It was."

They chatted with her teammates as Creed and Hope left the church and greeted guests in the vestibule. They'd all head to a restaurant, just out of town named, The Riverside Bar. Its simple name fooled everyone who walked in. It was a beautiful place located on the river. The outside decks allowed patrons to sit in rocking chairs and watch the river flow by on a nice warm day. Inside, it was the best wedding and banquet hall in town. A large dining area was transformed in minutes into a dance floor. A small stage up front held the bands that played.

Their row was allowed to leave and they stepped into the vestibule where the wedding party lined up. It was a small wedding. Only Falcon and Kori stood up with them because they said they needed the entire RAPTOR group with them and didn't know where to draw the line with such short notice. They opted for only Falcon and Kori and everyone else sat up front where the families sat since neither of them had many family members in attendance.

Hope's parents were there, her brother unable to get leave. Creed's parents were there, his brother and sister unable to make it in time with promises to come visit soon. They'd only set the date two weeks ago.

She hugged Falcon tightly then stood back. "You look very handsome in a tux Falcon."

His cheeks heated. "Shut up."

She laughed and hugged Kori. "How are you feeling today?"

"Better now. I think I ate a whole box of crackers downstairs though."

"It'll get better soon."

"I hope so. I don't think the grocery store has any more crackers left and Falcon is going to have to start driving hundreds of miles to find them."

She laughed at her friend and Kori blushed. Falcon kissed the top of her head. "I'll drive anywhere you need me to honey."

Emmy smiled at him and stepped up to Creed. "You look very handsome and very happy Creed. Congratulations."

"I am happy. Happier than I ever dreamed."

"It looks good on you."

Chase shook Creed's hand and she hugged Hope. "I'm happy for you Hope. You deserve to be happy."

"So do you."

She stepped back and looked Hope in the eyes and winked.

Chase hugged Hope then took Emmy's hand. "Want to take a walk?"

"Sure, we have a bit of time."

"Great. Follow me." He led her down the street and off to the right, a narrow hard-packed gravel road led them under a canopy of trees. "Wow, I didn't know this was here. It's beautiful."

He chuckled. "Diego told me about it."

"Really? How did he find it?"

Chase shrugged, "I guess he was running with Ted and Ted found it."

She laughed. "That's about right I guess."

They walked in silence. The peaceful setting healed something in her. It had been hectic the past few weeks. Casper called almost daily asking for reports. Names. Basic information they had gathered. Add to that, the wedding planning and frantic gathering of dresses and flowers and stuff had led to a hectic few weeks.

The birds serenaded them down the path, the only other sound was that of their footsteps crunching on the gravel. For the first time since her surgery, she noticed their footsteps were in perfect time. In the past, hers would have been uneven as she limped along. Her breathing faltered as she realized this newfound improvement in her body.

At the end of the clearing sat a beautiful pond.

"Oh, wow, that's fantastic."

"Isn't it? When I came down here yesterday morning I thought it was perfection."

"When did you come down here yesterday?"

"When I went for a run."

"That's a long run."

He grinned at her and shrugged. "Eight point four miles."

She laughed. "Wow."

He tugged her hand and led her to a small spot to the right. He let go of her hand and held up his finger for her to wait.

Bending, he reached under a shrub and pulled out a wicker basket. He opened the basket and pulled out a blanket and laid it on the ground.

He came to her and held his hand out. She put her hand in his and he escorted her to the blanket. "A seat for you madam."

She giggled and gracefully sat with her legs straight out in front of her. The champagne-colored satin slacks she wore reflected the waning sun's rays and she marveled at how pretty they looked.

Chase sat next to her and reached into the basket again. He pulled a bottle of wine from inside and produced two wine glasses.

She laughed. "Oh my gosh. What have you done?"

He chuckled. "I wanted you alone for a few minutes. We're hardly ever alone Em."

"We're alone in our room."

"Where we've both been so tired we barely say ten words before we drift off to sleep."

"We still find time to make love."

He leaned in and kissed her lips softly. "Thank God for that."

She laughed and took the glass of wine he held out to her.

They tapped their glasses gently together and took a drink. They both sat in silence for a few minutes, as a family of ducks peacefully floated by. She let her breathing even out and her shoulders relax and she realized just how hectic it had been.

"This is heavenly."

"I agree."

He set his glass on a flat rock to his right and turned to face her. He rose up on one knee and smiled at her.

"Emersyn Copeland. I couldn't do anything super romantic like take you back to where we met, because I don't have clearance to get us on base anymore."

She laughed as she stared into his handsome face. "I couldn't take you back to the hospital where we met again, because that isn't romantic."

She continued laughing as she watched his beaming smile.

"But I found this place and thought we'd come here to celebrate the exciting things in our life moving forward. The new things. The fun things. Or, just when we need to capture a few moments of peace and quiet."

He reached into his shirt pocket and pulled a ring from inside. "Emersyn Copeland, will you do me the honor of being my wife?"

She smiled and swallowed the knot that had instantly formed, then inhaled a deep breath. "I absolutely will be your wife."

His smile was sweet and reverent as he placed the beautiful ring on her finger. She watched it sparkle in the sunlight just before he leaned in and kissed her lips. They enjoyed each other's lips, molding, tasting, shaping as their tongues mated with each other. She inhaled his scent and she felt his heat as he held her close. He pulled back slightly and stared into her eyes.

"I love you Em."

She giggled and touched the side of his face. "I love you too."

Do you love the GHOST and RAPTOR families? Finding Lara, Book One in the GHOST Legacy series, is Gaige and Sophie Vickers son, Tate Vickers' story as he finds love with small town bakery owner, Lara Finley. Get your copy of Finding Lara here.

EPILOGUE

Chase's fingertips held Kori's wrist as he looked at his watch and counted her heartbeats.

"Okay, Kori. You're going to have to push on this next one."

Kori groaned loudly and he looked into Falcon's eyes, as he held his wife in a sitting position. Sweat trickled down Falcon's face but he'd been a trooper.

Kori squealed. "Another one."

Kori groaned and grunted as she pushed during this contraction and Falcon breathed out loud with her. She grunted once more and inhaled a deep breath. Then her face scrunched and she began pushing.

"The head's out Kori. Great job. Next contraction we'll birth the shoulders."

Kori huffed and leaned in against Falcon as she heaved large breaths in and out. Falcon kissed her temple. "You're doing great."

She only closed her eyes. Much to her credit, she didn't swear at Falcon like many women did to their husbands. But she wasn't in the mood for small talk, that was a fact.

Kori rose up, "Again." She began pushing and he helped the shoulders move out.

Once the second shoulder escaped the birth canal, the baby slid out and Chase caught it in his waiting arms.

"You have a beautiful baby girl."

Kori laughed. "Oh my god. A girl. Falcon, we have a daughter."

"I see her honey."

Chase placed the baby girl on Kori's chest and a nurse quickly wrapped a blanket around her. The tiny baby cried out and Kori laughed as she laid her hands on her new baby.

He looked up at Falcon and saw tears streaming down his cheeks as he looked at his little girl.

Chase had to finish delivering the afterbirth and get out of there. A nurse worked with Falcon to cut the umbilical cord.

He quickly finished up, then stood as he removed his gloves. "I'm sorry you two, I've got to go."

They both laughed. Kori shooed him away. "Go and tell Emmy we love her and congratulations. I'm sorry we'll miss it."

He waved as he left the room, nurses were there cleaning up. He hurried down the corridors of the hospital.

Jumping in his truck he raced from the parking lot and tapped the call button on his steering wheel. The robotic voice asked him for a command and he said, "Call Emmy."

"Calling Emmy." He listened as the phone rang on the other end. His eyes glanced at the clock. Ten minutes to go.

"Hi. Where are you?"

"I'm on my way. Ten minutes."

"Okay. And Kori?"

"They have a baby girl."

"Oh, that's just awesome. Do you know her name?"

"No honey, I rushed out to get to you on time."

She sighed. "Thank you. I'll see you in ten minutes."

"Yep."

The call ended and he put both hands on the wheel and pushed the gas pedal down a tiny bit further.

Finally pulling into the parking lot, he screeched to a halt, jumped from his truck, and ran to the back door of the building, which would take him to the basement. His pace didn't slow as he ran down the hallway to the room at the end. He pushed open the door and saw Isaac first.

"It's about time Chase."

"I know. Where's my tux?"

"It's over here. Come on, I'll help you."

He walked across the room to his tuxedo, hanging on a coat rack. Diego stood when he walked in. "Well?"

"Girl."

"Awesome. What's her name?"

"I don't know Diego, I literally ran out of the room."

"Okay."

Diego's phone buzzed and he looked at it and laughed. "Her name is Oakleigh."

Creed laughed. "That's an awesome name."

Chase hurried into his tuxedo, the sweat still running down his face. "Do I smell? I think I smell."

Isaac laughed at him and handed him deodorant from a toiletry bag he had on the table.

"Good thinking."

"I figured you'd be hustling."

He swabbed on the deodorant and buttoned up his shirt. He stepped into the shoes Isaac set at his feet and popped the cuff links into his shirt cuffs.

He took in a deep breath and looked around the room. The RAPTOR men were here. They'd decided everyone needed to be in the wedding, plus Isaac. So their attendants were standing up with their husbands and wives, and Isaac's wife stood in for Kori. Emmy's brother, Hayden, stood in for Falcon. It all worked out, everyone was included.

"Okay. I'm ready." Isaac turned and looked at him, smiled, and nodded. "You sure are. Let's go get you married."

He eagerly nodded. When Kori went into labor this morning, he thought about backing out of delivering her baby, but he'd made her a promise. Emmy told him to go and deliver the baby as he'd promised, and they'd get married when he finished. They were so fortunate Kori breezed through labor.

He walked with his new friends, and old friend, up the stairs to the back room behind the altar. The minister was there waiting for them and nodded when Chase and company walked in.

"Are you ready Chase?"

"Yes sir."

The minister nodded. "Gentlemen, make your way to the entryway to find your bridesmaid."

After they left, he shook Chase's hand. "Good luck to you son."

"Thank you."

The minister held his hand out toward the door that led them to the altar and walked out first. The pianist began playing an introduction, then Chase stepped out and took his place at the altar to await his bride.

The pianist changed the song once more and the wedding march officially began.

Chase's heart beat a steady rhythm. It had finally slowed, and he'd stopped sweating. The first couple walked toward him, Deacon and Becca. They smiled as they neared, Deacon kissed Becca sweetly before they parted and took their places on opposite sides of the altar.

Donovan and Hadleigh walked up next. Both looked glamorous in their finery, both wore smiles on their faces.

Caiden and Mia came after and glanced at each other often as they walked down the aisle. Caiden nodded when he stepped past him and shook his hand.

Royce and Piper were next. A few of the congregation whispered as they walked past. Royce was well-known all around the US after his stint with the Las Vegas Sinners and the dirty dealings that happened in that town. To his credit, he laid his right hand over Piper's resting on his left arm and only had eyes for her.

Charly and Sam were next. Charly's very round baby belly was prominent, her and Sam's smiles were unmatched. Emmy was right, Charly was hard to forget.

Diego and Shelby made their way toward him next, and Diego grinned broadly at him as he neared, Chase grinned from ear to ear.

Creed and Hope came next. Their smiles were wide as they neared him. They had just announced her pregnancy last week.

Hayden, and Isaac's wife, Louise, neared him and he smiled at both of them. They both beamed at him and separated to their places.

Isaac and Emmy's sister, Elise, walked down the aisle last and Chase stifled the frustration of having to stand with this silly grin on his face for all of their friends when all he wanted was to see Emmy.

The music changed then, the congregation stood, and finally, his beautiful bride, Emmy, and her parents began walking toward him. She was sensational in her dress. Her sleek satin dress fit her curves perfectly, her long dark hair curled down around her shoulders like a dark cloud. She wore a simple tiara on her head, and he couldn't have picked anything more perfect than that look for her. She was perfection.

They stopped before him, and he shook Dane's hand as Emmy hugged her mom. Then he stepped around her and hugged Keirnan before turning to Emmy and smiling at her. "You are stunning."

She chuckled. "I've been sweating."

"God, me too."

They both laughed and walked up the two steps to stand before the minister to become husband and wife.

Do you love the GHOST and RAPTOR families? Finding Lara, Book One in the GHOST Legacy series, is Gaige and Sophie Vickers son, Tate Vickers' story as he finds love with small town bakery owner, Lara Finley. Get your copy of Finding Lara here.

ALSO BY PJ FIALA

To see a list of all of my books with the blurbs go to:
https://www.pjfiala.com/bibliography-pj-fiala/

You can find all of my books at https://pjfiala.com/books

Romantic Suspense

Rolling Thunder Series

Moving to Love, Book 1

Moving to Hope, Book 2

Moving to Forever, Book 3

Moving to Desire, Book 4

Moving to You, Book 5

Moving Home, Book 6

Moving On, Book 7

Rolling Thunder Boxset, Books 1-3

Military Romantic Suspense

Second Chances Series

Designing Samantha's Love, Book 1

Securing Kiera's Love, Book 2

Second Chances Boxset - Duet

Bluegrass Security Series

Heart Thief, Book One

Finish Line, Book Two

Lethal Love, Book Three

Wrenched Fate, Book Four

Bluegrass Security Boxset, Books 1-3

Big 3 Security

Ford: Finding His Fire Book One

Lincoln: Finding His Mark Book Two

Dodge: Finding His Jewel Book Three

Rory: Finding His Match Book Four

Big 3 Security Boxset, Books 1-3

GHOST

Defending Keirnan, GHOST Book One

Defending Sophie, GHOST Book Two

Defending Roxanne, GHOST Book Three

Defending Yvette, GHOST Book Four

Defending Bridget, GHOST Book Five

Defending Isabella, GHOST Book Six

RAPTOR

RAPTOR Rising - Prequel

Saving Shelby, RAPTOR Book One

Holding Hadleigh, RAPTOR Book Two

Craving Charlesia, RAPTOR Book Three

Promising Piper, RAPTOR Book Four

Missing Mia, RAPTOR Book Five

Believing Becca, RAPTOR Book Six

Keeping Kori, RAPTOR Book Seven

Healing Hope, RAPTOR Book Eight

Engaging Emersyn, RAPTOR Book Nine

GHOST Legacy (Next generation)

Finding Lara, Book One

Saving Elena, Book Two

Rescuing Kenna, Book Three

Protecting Everleigh, Book Four

Guarding Adelaide, Book Five

Shielding Maya, Book Six

MEET PJ

Writing has been a desire my whole life. Once I found the courage to write, life changed for me in the most profound way. Bringing stories to readers that I'd enjoy reading and creating characters that are flawed, but lovable is such a joy.

When not writing, I'm with my family doing something fun. My husband, Gene, and I are bikers and enjoy riding to new locations, meeting new people and generally enjoying this fabulous country we live in.

I come from a family of veterans. My grandfather, father, brother, two sons, and one daughter-in-law are all veterans. Needless to say, I am proud to be an American and proud of the service my amazing family has given.

My online home is https://www.pjfiala.com.
You can connect with me on Facebook: https://www.facebook.com/PJFiala1,
Instagram: https://www.Instagram.com/PJFiala
Tiktok: https://www.tiktok.com/@pjfiala?lang=en .
If you prefer to email, go ahead, I'll respond - pjfiala@pjfiala.com.

Made in the USA
Columbia, SC
25 November 2022

72086275R00161